Other books by Garth Wallace

Fly Yellow Side Up
Pie In The Sky
Derry Air
Cockpit Follies
The Flying Circus
If Clouds Could Talk
You'd Fly Laughing Too

Don't Call Me a Legend
Blue Collar Pilots

Library and Archives Canada Cataloguing in Publication

Wing Nuts
fiction, humour, aviation, flying

Written by: Garth Wallace

ISBN 0-9739214-1-2

    I. Title.

PS8595.A56516W55 2006   C813'.54   C2006-905809-1

Cover and inside artwork: Francois Bougie, Bizzart

Editing: Liz Wallace, Sari Funston & Francois Bougie

Layout and typesetting: Happy Landings Publishing

Written, illustrated, typeset, printed and bound in Canada
Published October, 2006

Published by:

**Happy Landings
851 Heritage Dr. RR #4
Merrickville, Ontario
Canada K0G 1N0
Tel.: 613-269-2552
Fax: 613-269-3962
E-mail: books@happylandings.com
Web site: www.happylandings.com**

Contents

Introduction
Dedication
Chapter One – Cheeky devils
Chapter Two – Snappy
Chapter Three – Galley slaves
Chapter Four – Icabod
Chapter Five – Summer 1, Larry 0
Chapter Six – Stuffed
Chapter Seven – Leftovers
Chapter Eight – Sex and self-defence
Chapter Nine – Idiot proof
Chapter Ten – Surprise!
Chapter Eleven – Pheasant Island
Chapter Twelve – Medevac
Chapter Thirteen – The test
Chapter Fourteen – Hop-a-long Hathaway
Chapter Fifteen – The gigolo
Chapter Sixteen – The deal
Chapter Seventeen – Call God
Chapter Eighteen – Spun
Chapter Nineteen – Double talk
Chapter Twenty – In the flesh
Chapter Twenty-one – "Yes, sir."
Chapter Twenty-two – My place
Chapter Twenty-three – The Motivator
Chapter Twenty-four – Robot
Chapter Twenty-five – New girl
Chapter Twenty-six – A tale of two classes
Chapter Twenty-seven – Looped

Wing Nuts

Graham, all the best! Garth

by Garth Wallace

Illustrated by Francois Bougie

Chapter Twenty-eight – "Yes!"
Chapter Twenty-nine – Melville
Chapter Thirty – "Beer?"
Chapter Thirty-one – Looking up
Chapter Thirty-two – Above and Beyond

*The Cub obediently staggered
into the air at 40 mph.*

Introduction

Local airports attract the fun lovers, the doers, the adventurous and the eccentrics from all walks of life. I worked as a flying instructor at small air services. I'd go to work smiling just to meet the next wing nut who came through the door. If laughter is the best medicine, I should live a long time.

Garth Wallace
October, 2006

Dedication

Wing Nuts *is dedicated to the Jim and Leslie Kings of the world; the kind of people who make it better.*

Happy Landings Publishing
Our readers laugh

Chapter One

Cheeky devils

A thin, awkward-looking man shoved the door open and stumbled into the flying school office. He turned and frowned at the entrance as if it had snagged him on purpose.

The stranger's face and limbs looked like they had been assembled by a team of doctors who couldn't agree. He stood on lopsided legs. His stubby nose was bent to the right pulling his mouth with it. One misplaced eye focused on me; the other pointed at the ceiling.

There were three of us in the room. Our receptionist, Leanne Rains, was seated at her desk behind the counter. I was at a table to one side briefing a student pilot before taking him on a flying lesson. We stopped what we were doing and stared at the newcomer.

Leanne stood up. "Hi! Welcome to The Flying Circus," she said cheerfully. "May I help you?"

The man pretended not to hear her. "Are you the guy in charge?" he asked me. His words whistled out his mouth and nose.

"Yes," Leanne replied from behind him.

He frowned and continued to focus an eye on me. "I'm Cameron Shuttlecock, the photographer," he announced. "I'm here about renting your Super Cub."

"Well, Mr. Shuttlecock," Leanne answered pleasantly, "we're always happy to have new customers. Is this for a charter trip or a local flight?"

"It's for aerial photography," he grumbled impatiently. He was trying his chauvinistic best to ignore the receptionist.

She wasn't letting him. She walked around the counter toward the entrance as she spoke. "When would you like to book this flight, sir?" she asked.

"Now, of course! That's why I'm here!" the twitchy man said in a raised voice. He was still talking to me.

"For aerial photography, of course," he grumbled.

"We don't have a pilot for you right away, Mr. Shuttlecock," Leanne said, closing the front door, "but we could arrange something for this afternoon." She headed back to the counter.

"I want to fly tomorrow, not today!" he barked. He was sounding frustrated.

Leanne possessed savvy that was hidden by her mild manner and modest appearance. She had taught inner city public school while raising two hellions at home. Now she worked at a struggling air service owned by her husband and me. Leanne's friendliness never wavered but aviation had more than its share of spoiled males. She rarely missed a chance to drive a stake into chauvinism.

Our receptionist was now standing next to the man. She flipped the pages on the booking sheets. I turned my attention back to my student.

"I think I understand, Mr. Shuttlecock," Leanne continued. "You'd like to book the Super Cub and a pilot now, for tomorrow." She was sounding more patient than our visitor.

"Isn't that what I said?" he answered loudly.

"What time tomorrow, sir?" she asked. She lowered her voice so it was difficult to hear her.

Shuttlecock half turned toward Leanne. "From nine until eleven!" he declared.

Leanne said quietly. "That will be $65 per hour."

I looked up again. She was quoting ten dollars over our regular rate. I knew our Super Cub was underutilized during the weekdays. Floating around in the slow-flying airplane while this wing nut snapped pictures seemed like easy money. Maybe I could work something out with him.

At that moment Leanne gave me a "don't-you-dare" look.

"That's too much!" Shuttlecock barked. "I'll have to teach the pilot how to fly aerial photography. I'll pay $45 per hour for the airplane and I won't charge for the lessons."

"The price is $65 an hour," Leanne answered calmly.

The door opened and Henry Rains, Leanne's husband, walked in with a student pilot. Shuttlecock turned his attention to him immediately.

"I'm Cameron Shuttlecock, the photographer," he announced. "I'm booking the Super Cub and a pilot for aerial photos tomorrow. We were establishing the price. Maybe you can help us."

Henry looked at Leanne. She flashed him the same glare that she had given me. The difficult man didn't see it.

"Well, Mr. Shuttlecock," Henry replied kindly, "I'm pleased to meet you. My name is Henry Rains." He reached out and offered a handshake.

Shuttlecock took it with a right hand that appeared to be a few fingers short.

Henry motioned toward his wife. "I'm sure Leanne can arrange whatever you need. I'll just finish with my student."

"I'll wait!" the photographer snapped.

Henry was tall, fair-haired, medium-sized and well liked. He treated people with understanding and fairness, legacies from growing up on the Canadian prairies. He tended to be quiet but was not shy.

"Suit yourself, sir, but I'll be a while. Leanne can make a booking for you and take your deposit."

"What about the price?" Shuttlecock demanded.

Henry glanced at his wife again. She thrust her chin forward. I recognized it as another "back-off" warning signal.

"Mr. Shuttlecock," Henry replied, "Leanne pays our bills. She's the one authorized to set prices but I'm sure you'll get your money's worth with us."

"Humph!" the photographer snorted. He turned toward Leanne and stamped his feet in anger. He aimed his wandering eyes on either side of our receptionist rather than focus on her.

"Book me for tomorrow from nine until eleven!" he ordered.

"That will be $65," Leanne replied. "The balance is payable following the flight."

The grumpy photographer pulled out a wallet on a chain, yanked out a credit card and slapped it on the counter. "Who will be the pilot?" he asked loudly.

Leanne checked the booking sheets again, smiled and then announced clearly, "Oh, I guess it will be me!"

Chapter Two

Snappy

"Harry Bottom the Third, this is Sierra Charlie Uniform Bravo, do you read?"

Shuttlecock the photographer was calling a ship from the back seat of the Piper Super Cub.

I was flying.

There was no reply.

We were at 4,500 feet over Lake Erie. Our headsets were plugged into a marine radio through the airplane's intercom. Snappy repeated his transmission to the ship.

"Harry Bottom the Third, this is Sierra Charlie Uniform Bravo, do you read?"

Leanne had been pulling Shuttlecock's chauvinist leg when she announced that she would be his pilot. Our receptionist was not a flier but she had let the difficult man rant a bit before telling him.

"I'm not flying with any woman!" he declared.

"Oh come now, Mr. Shuttlecock. I'm not just any woman."

"I... I don't care w... what you are!" he sputtered. "I... I'll never f... fly with a female!"

The contorted man was about to storm out in frustration.

"I'm joking," Leanne explained. "I run the office and let the men do the flying."

There was a long pause while Shuttlecock focused an eye on Leanne for the first time. She smiled sweetly.

He pointed a crooked finger at the appointment sheets. "Are you saying that you're booking me with a man?" he asked in a less elevated tone.

"I've booked you to fly with a pilot," Leanne answered, still smiling. "I'm not a pilot."

"Are... are all your pilots men?"

"One is for sure," she replied happily, "the others I haven't checked."

Shuttlecock tried a smile. His cock-eyed mouth twisted his features further out of shape. "You are a cheeky devil," he said from one side of his face.

Leanne laughed. "That makes two of us."

The next morning, I had the Super Cub out, fueled and ready to go when Shuttlecock arrived in a hurry. He drove his Land Rover through the parking lot, across the grass, over the garden and onto the ramp in front of our hangar. He stopped beside the airplane and jumped out wearing a full camouflage suit. I had not been looking forward to flying with the potentially prickly man. Now he was dressed for a covert operation. I didn't know what to think.

"Good morning, Mr. Shuttlecock," I said with forced cheerfulness.

"Call me Snappy!" he replied, diving into the back of the Land Rover. He sounded like he wanted to be friendly but didn't know how.

He pulled out two red life jackets and threw one at me. "Put this on," he said. "If you screw up over the lake, you'll need it."

The bulky vest sailed past me out of reach. He must have been aiming with one eye and throwing with the other. I walked over, picked it up and slipped it on.

"Should I be wearing fatigues?" I asked.

He frowned.

I pointed to his clothes.

"Pockets," he answered. "Photographers need lots of pockets."

I helped him load two cameras along with a large soft-sided case of accessories and a portable marine radio into the Cub. The equipment filled the small baggage compartment behind the cockpit.

"OK, let's get cracking," he said and scampered into the back seat.

The Land Rover sat with its doors open blocking the ramp. I stood beside the Cub until one of Snappy's eyes looked up again.

"Let's go!" he said impatiently. "Time is money!"

"Are the keys in the Rover?" I asked.

He furrowed his brow and looked at the car. He slapped eight different pockets in his suit and said, "They must be."

"I'll move it," I said.

"Right!"

Now Shuttlecock was trying to raise the ship's crew on the marine radio to let them know we were inbound. There was still no reply from his second transmission.

"I'll try something else," he said to me. "Harry Bottom, Charlie Uniform Bravo is an airplane flying 20 miles to your northeast to rendezvous for a photo shoot requested by the company president, over."

A few moments later a rough-sounding seaman's voice came on the frequency. "Is there an airplane calling the Harry Bottom?"

"Affirmative, Harry Bottom, this is Charlie Uniform Bravo, a small airplane 20 miles northeast inbound for a photo shoot as requested by company headquarters, over."

There was a pause.

"We don't know about any photo shoot," the voice growled.

"The ship was contacted about us coming," Snappy complained to me over the intercom. "The crew is lazy. They don't want to be bothered by someone taking pictures.

"Harry Bottom, this is Charlie Uniform Bravo, may I speak to the captain please?"

"The captain is busy, Airplane Charlie."

"Roger, Harry Bottom, we can wait but the sun is at the right angle now for a nice big photo of the Harry Bottom to hang in the company boardroom."

Another pause.

A deeper voice came on the frequency. "Airplane calling the Harry Bottom, this is the captain."

"Good morning captain, Cameron Shuttlecock here. We have been commissioned by your headquarters to shoot aerial portrait photos of your ship, over."

"Standby."

"Standing by," Snappy replied.

"He's probably checking with his dispatcher," he said to me. "Start descending while we're waiting and keep the speed up."

"Roger," I replied.

I commenced a pre-descent check: fuel on fullest tank, magnetos on both, mixture rich, engine oil temperature and pressure in the green, carburetor heat checked, seat belts fastened.

The captain came back on the radio. "Airplane calling the Harry Bottom, take your pictures but remain well away from the ship."

"Thank you, sir. I have one more request."

"Go ahead."

"The visibility up here is not very good. Would you have your radar angled up to track us? We are descending out of 4,500 feet and would appreciate a range and bearing to the ship."

"Standby."

"Standing by."

"Airplane Charlie, we have a small target bearing 005, range 18 miles."

"That's us," Snappy said cheerfully. "We'll call again in a few minutes, Charlie Uniform Bravo, out."

He tapped me vigorously on the shoulder. "Turn toward the ship and go down," he said, impatiently stabbing a finger toward the lake.

"Yes, sir."

I turned the airplane to the left, reduced the power and eased the stick forward.

It was a warm, humid day in May. The pollution-laden, moist air around the industrialized Great Lakes Region of North America made it look like we were flying in pea soup. The visibility at our altitude was three miles in haze, at best. I was staring into a murky sky that blended into the calm, grey waters of Lake Erie. The Super Cub was equipped with instruments to help pilots stay right side up in those conditions but it did not have electronic navigation aids.

Snappy had phoned the shipping company before our departure. He had been given the Harry Bottom's position as 15 miles east of Long Point. The ship was headed for Port Colburne, the Lake Erie entrance to the Welland Canal. From there she would travel through the locks to Lake Ontario and on to the steel mills in Hamilton with a load of iron ore.

I had navigated by map to Lake Erie's north shore from our home base at the Circus Airport. From there I flew an estimated heading toward the ship. The chances of us finding her were remote without bearings from the crew's radar.

Our position to the Harry Bottom was 185 degrees according to the captain. The ship was steaming from our right to left. The wind was calm. I flew a course of 185 degrees deciding that it was better to miss her from behind. We could spot her wake and follow it up her stern.

Five minutes later I leveled off at 2,000 feet. I couldn't see anything ahead but featureless water and matching sky.

Snappy pulled himself forward on my seatback and looked over my shoulder.

"Harry Bottom, this is airplane Charlie Uniform Bravo," he said into his microphone. "What is our present bearing from the ship for a heading check, over?"

A few moments later, the seaman's voice came over the radio, "Airplane Charlie, bearing 002 degrees, range eight miles."

"Thank you Harry Bottom. We should see you shortly," the photographer replied. He tapped my shoulder with a crooked finger and pointed left.

I corrected a few degrees and stared into the grey beyond. Soon a dark shape appeared in the gloom straight ahead and slightly below us. It looked like a toy ship suspended in space. Its black hull trailed a widening "V" of wake.

"That's her," Snappy declared, still leaning forward. "We'll circle and take some overhead shots."

"Yes, sir."

The toy rapidly grew into a large freighter riding low in the water.

I pulled the power back, slowed the airplane and lowered full flap. I called out my checklist: "Aircraft radio on emergency frequency 121.5, seatbelts tight, flaps down, speed 65 mph and door open."

"I'm ready for the door," Snappy said.

I clamped the control stick between my knees, twisted to my right and unlatched the Cub's split door. I eased the bottom half down against the fuselage and pushed the top half up into a latch under the wing. Snappy leaned toward the opening holding a small, 35mm camera at the ready. Cool air blasted in through the open side of the fuselage. It missed me but hit my passenger. His fatigues were done up under his lifejacket and his

"Turn… more bank… more! No, not so tight!"

baseball cap was turned around and held down by his headset.

"Harry Bottom, this is Airplane Charlie," Snappy said on the radio. He had to shout over the wind noise. "You should see us overhead."

A microphone clicked twice on the frequency. It was the only acknowledgement.

I positioned the Cub with the ship on our right and circled it in a gentle bank. Snappy leaned into the slipstream with the 35mm camera against his face. The wind activated his microphone and roared through the intercom. He shouted corrections over the noise.

"Turn… more bank… more! No, not so tight!"

At one point the darkened silhouette of the ship passed through a shimmering reflection of the sun on the water. I could hear the camera's autowind buzzing over the intercom on top of the other noises.

"Stop right there!" Snappy yelled.

I smiled at the impossible command and held the controls in place.

He leaned back a few moments later. "Take us down for low-level work," he barked.

I set up a spiral descent until we were approaching the ship's bow, right side to right side. We were about 1,000 feet away and 100 feet off the water. I already knew from my briefing with Snappy on the way that he had no intention of staying well clear of the ship. "Portraits are not shot from a distance," he had said.

Giant white letters spelled "Lake Land Shipping" along the hull. The Harry Bottom was one of the older freighter designs. The bridge superstructure was mounted on the bow while the engine-room and accommodations were built aft. A long deck with rows of red hatch covers separated them.

Snappy aimed his camera. "Too far away!" he bellowed.

I dipped the right wing and side slipped the Cub closer.

"Too far along!" Snappy barked. "They don't want pictures of half a ship!" He slumped back into his seat.

We flew past three men watching us from the railing on the deck above the engine rooms. I waved. They didn't wave back.

I could see that Snappy would have to be quick on these close-in shots. The closing speed between the Cub and the ship made for a rapidly changing view.

The stern of the ship disappeared behind the right wing. The hull was my only reference for level flight above the calm surface of the lake. I shifted my concentration to the instrument panel and carefully turned around to the right. I leaned forward to catch the ship reappearing in that side of the windshield.

I rolled out of the turn and lifted the right wing. The Harry Bottom was almost underneath us. I pushed the left rudder pedal and slipped the plane sideways to position Snappy's view of the ship ahead of the struts and behind the arc of the propeller. This presented him with the ship's left side, stern first, silhouetted against the sun.

"Wing up!" he barked from the door opening. "More! I'm seeing propeller arc. We're in too tight!"

I moved the controls in response to his commands. The Cub wiggled along the length of the freighter toward the bow.

He snapped one shot of the silhouette. "Take me around to the other side," he ordered.

Then he radioed the ship. "Harry Bottom, this is Charlie Uniform Bravo, please send the three seamen on the starboard railing inside until we are done."

"Click, click," the ship replied.

"Lower on the next pass," Snappy called out to me.

I flew beyond the bow, descended and then circled cautiously for a pass along the ship's right side. We were 50 feet off the water. I lifted the right wing and pushed right rudder to keep the ship in Snappy's view.

He clicked away and shouted commands, "Nose left! More left!"

He was asking the impossible. With the right wing up, the Cub wanted to turn away from the ship. Right rudder stopped the turn but pulled the propeller arc toward the ship. I eased off the rudder pedal and let the airplane turn slightly.

"Hold it! Hold it!"

There were no seamen at the railing.

Snappy called the ship at the end of that pass. "Harry Bottom, we need you to run some colourful flags up the signaling mast but nothing obscene or we'll all be in trouble."

A microphone clicked an acknowledgement.

"Stay wide on your turnaround," Snappy said to me. "I want to change cameras."

I flew a big circle on instruments. I could feel the photographer shifting around in the back seat. He was digging out his Hasselblad aerial camera from the baggage compartment behind him. It was the size of a breadbox with airplane-like control handles on each side. It used glass plates for film.

"This camera is worth over $20,000," he shouted. "The plates are expensive. We make every shot count. Let's go."

I turned toward the ship. I could see a string of tiny colourful flags being hoisted up the signaling mast above the bridge. I thought it was interesting that the gruff-sounding crew would obey this pesky photographer so easily. Next, he'll be steering the ship, I said to myself.

"Lower!" he yelled.

I dropped us down to 25 feet, rolled out of the turn and raised the right

"Take us down and fly low and in tight to the ship's starboard side."

wing. The Harry Bottom was steaming straight at us at eye level. The ramp of water being pushed up by the round bow was a display of enormous size and power.

The Hasselblad had a look-down viewfinder. Snappy had to lean further into the slipstream to line up the big camera. He pressed the right side of his face into the rubber eyepiece. His errant left eye stared at me. He snapped a picture and then hurriedly slapped in a new plate. I let the Cub side slip clear of the oncoming ship.

"More wing up!" he yelled.

I added left bank and right rudder. He kept the propeller out of the pictures by leaning further out of the door opening.

He'll be really mad if he drops that camera, I thought to myself. Then I realized that he couldn't lean that far out without unbuckling his seatbelt. He took another photo. I instinctively banked more to the left to keep him from falling out. He leaned further. His body was outside the cabin down to his waist. I switched my left hand onto the control stick and grabbed the back of his belt with my right.

"Wing down!" he bellowed.

I dropped the wing slightly and tightened my grip.

He took a picture and retreated back to his seat. I pulled my hand out of his belt.

"What are you doing?" he frowned.

"I didn't want to lose you."

"Don't worry. If I go in, I'll keep shooting."

I believed him.

"Take us up to 500 feet and get ready for more overheads."

"Yes, sir." I added power.

"Harry Bottom, we need more sun on the right side. Please alter course 60 degrees to starboard and hold it for five minutes, then turn port 120 so we can shoot the other side, over."

After a long pause, the radio replied, "Roger."

I couldn't believe that the captain would steer this expensive monster off course on a photographer's request. The ship slowly began to turn.

I circled. Snappy was shooting down so he didn't have to lean out as far. He exposed two plates, one where I tried to position the ship and its curving wake into the sun's shimmering reflection. I could only guess if Snappy was getting what he wanted in his viewfinder.

"How was that?" I asked.

"Take us down and fly low and in tight to the ship's starboard side."

He was saying, "Please," to the ship's crew but not to me.

"Yes, sir," I replied.

I descended to 20 feet and flew toward the ship's right front quarter. I lifted the right wing and started a gentle left turn.

"Lower!" Snappy barked.

I milked the Cub down to ten feet. We were now looking up at the black side of a freighter that was riding low in the water. I couldn't see the deck.

"Wing up!" he shouted and leaned out ahead of the strut.

I switched hands, grabbed his belt and banked some more. I watched the water's surface carefully. I realized that Lake Erie was not completely calm. Long flat rollers made the surface rise and fall. We passed the ship. I pulled back on the stick to put more airspace under us.

Snappy sat back. I retrieved my right hand.

"Up to 500 feet again," he demanded. He said nothing about my helpful grasp.

"Harry Bottom," he radioed, "now the other side, please."

We climbed. The ship turned. I had trouble placing the target in the sun's reflection. My passenger complained loudly.

"No, no! In the sun! The sun! That big bright thing over there!"

He didn't get a good shot.

"Forget it! Take us down. We're shooting the ship's left side and make sure the pass is low this time!"

I checked the airplane's systems and instruments, switched fuel tanks and descended. We were approaching the Harry Bottom from her right stern quarter as she was coming out of her turn. We were flying between five and ten feet above the surface depending on our position over each roller. I crabbed the Cub with the right wing up, added power and switched hands on the stick. Snappy stretched forward. I hooked my right hand over his belt. He looked down into the camera.

"Lower!" he yelled over the intercom.

I didn't dare.

"Lower!" he screamed.

I eased the Cub down a couple of feet. We were at the perfect place for a full-length photo of the ship with the stern superstructure towering in the foreground.

Snappy bent further forward. I held onto him while gingerly working the stick.

"Lower, damn it!"

I was doing my best but he was dictating the impossible.

I eased forward on the control stick and aimed for the crest of the next roller. The devil made me do it. I braced myself and tightened my grip on Snappy's belt. The left tire smacked the surface of the lake. The Cub lurched. Water splashed up everywhere. We skipped into the air.

Chapter Three

Galley slaves

"Major Airlines is hiring pilots," Larry Tragunno said. The comment slid out casually.

Larry was a former flying instructor who had made the leap to airline flying. The big man with a deep voice often visited The Flying Circus when we were grounded by bad weather. Bantering with old workmates allowed Larry to relive the camaraderie of his teaching days without having to actually fly with students. He also enjoyed dangling the prospect of working for the big leagues in front of other pilots.

"I have a job already," I replied.

Larry glanced out the window. "Not today, you don't."

He was right. Henry Rains, Larry and I were sipping coffee, swapping flying stories and watching the spring rain wash out our training flights.

"Come on, Larry," I prodded, "you miss instructing, otherwise you wouldn't come here."

The airline pilot chuckled. "Yah, I really miss sitting around on rainy days, drinking bad coffee, having these stimulating conversations and not getting paid."

Henry smiled and nodded knowingly.

Larry's hiring news might have fallen on receptive ears six months earlier. The start-up of The Flying Circus had proven that two flying instructors could not succeed in their own air service on enthusiasm alone. Help from customers, suppliers and backstopping by Leanne had carried us through the slow growth, bad weather and financial terror of our first two years.

Now we had four airplanes on lease, including the Super Cub, and had built a hangar. Business had been picking up this spring. We had started towing banners in addition to our regular flight training, charter, sightseeing and corporate flying. Aerial photography had been another extra until I splashed Snappy Shuttlecock with Lake Erie. Still, the training starts were up. We were hoping to get ahead enough this summer to hire another pilot or two.

"Galley slaves deliver coffee just to spend time with the pilots."

"We might be looking for more instructors," I said to Larry. "How about renewing your rating?"

"Not on your life!"

"What's so great about being an airline pilot?" I asked.

Larry raised his cup in salute. "The coffee is better for starters and we get paid to drink it."

"You told me that the big salary didn't come until you made captain."

"It doesn't but I get paid three times my old instructing salary and all I do is show up and ride along. The airplanes fly themselves and sexy galley slaves deliver coffee just so they can spend time with the pilots."

"Whoa, that's big talk. I thought you said the stews on your routes were worn-out seniors."

Larry grinned. "I told you that's what I said to my wife."

Leanne Rains stood up from her chair behind the flight desk and walked toward the coffeemaker. She was the only one in the office doing any work. Personal experience gave me an idea of what was coming next. Henry realized it too.

Our receptionist picked up the half-filled pot of coffee from the burner and waved it at us. "Refills anyone?"

Henry and I jumped up. "Yes, please, Leanne," we chimed together. We took our mugs over to her.

"Yah, thanks Leanne," Larry said, leaning forward with his cup.

She poured the steaming liquid first into my mug and then Henry's. Then she stepped toward Larry. She tipped the pot up beside his outstretched hand and sloshed the coffee down his leg.

Larry screamed and leaped off the chesterfield. "What the...!" he exclaimed.

I had never heard his voice reach so high or seen him move so fast. He tried to shake the coffee-covered pants away from his skin. His dancing feet splashed in the mess on the floor. The remnants of coffee in his swinging cup sloshed onto his shirt.

"Damn!"

Leanne smiled. "The coffee here might not be as good as Major Airlines," she said, "but how do your rate the galley slaves?"

Larry was hopping around instead of responding. Leanne reached the pot over his head. He spoke just in time.

"Just as pretty!" he yelped.

"I think you're prettier," I declared.

"Yes, much better looking than any airline stewardesses," Henry added quickly.

Leanne stood down from her threatening pose. "Why thank you, gentlemen." Then she added, "The floor mop is in the washroom."

Henry went for the mop. I started moving furniture out of the way. Larry stopped dancing but kept his eye on Leanne. He leaned toward me.

"What got into her?" he whispered.

"You pushed the wrong button," I replied quietly. "You inferred that female cabin crews were born to serve coffee to male pilots."

"I didn't say that!"

"I know, but you came close enough."

Larry let out a long breath. "I didn't know Leanne was a such firecracker."

"Don't take it personally. She likes you, otherwise she would have dumped the coffee on your head."

"Sheesh, I can get that kind of respect at home."

"Welcome to The Flying Circus; populated by men, run by a woman."

Chapter Four

Icabod

We were mopping up coffee when there was a knock on the office door. Nobody reacted right away. Customers normally just walked in. Henry went over and opened the door.

A tall, skinny, young man was standing on the steps in the rain.

"Come in, come in," Henry said.

The stranger stepped over the threshold.

Henry offered a handshake. "Welcome to The Flying Circus. I'm Henry Rains."

The youngster stood with his head bowed. His dripping blond hair looked like it had been cut around a bowl. A large nose divided his freckled face. The waistband of his pants was hiked halfway up to his armpits under a heavy rubber coat. His bare ankles were planted in wooden shoes. He held out a wet hand and let Henry pump it a couple of times.

"What can I do for you?" Henry asked.

"Well, s... sir," the newcomer said haltingly, "I... I'm a commercial pilot and I want... ahh... a job teaching if... I take your instructor's course."

He did not look like any pilot that I had seen. He spoke as if someone had told him what to say but he hadn't rehearsed it enough.

"Good for you," Henry enthused. "We are well set up to teach instructors here." He placed a hand on the sputterer's wet shoulder. "Give me your coat and then come over to meet some folks and we'll talk."

Henry hung the rubber coat on a peg by the door. "Tell me your name," he asked.

The answer was barely audible. "Icabod Brimsmeade."

"Well, Icabod Brimsmeade," he said, steering the young man toward where Larry and I were pushing furniture back into place. "This is our chief pilot," Henry said introducing me, "and this is Larry Tragunno, a pilot with Major Airlines and our chief couch monkey."

"Hey, it's Captain Tragunno to you," Larry said.

"Sorry, this is Captain Couch Monkey."

Icabod looked so timid, I'm sure he'd have soiled himself if someone had popped a paper bag. Larry surveyed him like he was from outer space. The kid didn't step forward to shake hands so either did I.

"I'm pleased to meet you, Icabod," I said.

He glanced at me nervously but didn't reply.

"Have a seat," Henry offered, motioning toward the chesterfield. The youngster sat on the edge of the cushion.

"Would you like a cup of coffee?" Henry asked.

"Don't let Leanne to get it for you," Larry interjected.

Icabod shook his head back and forth vigorously. The rest of us took that as a "No," and sat down.

"Icabod is a commercial pilot," Henry explained, "who wants to take a flying instructor's course and teach, is that correct?"

The shy pilot nodded a "Yes".

"Where did you learn to fly?" Henry asked.

"At Princess College," he replied, avoiding eye contact.

"And you were wondering if you'd be hired as staff here after taking our instructor's course?"

"Yes," he said quietly. He seemed to relax slightly as Henry took the words he wanted to say out of his mouth.

"My... my professor at the college told us, ahh... to ask for work before paying for the course."

"He was right," Henry replied, "and you're doing just what he suggested." He paused for a moment. Icabod relaxed a little more.

I tried to kick Henry's foot but it was out of reach. I didn't want him to promise this strange youngster any work. I frowned and moved my head back and forth. Henry ignored me.

"What did your professor suggest if you didn't like instructing?" Henry asked.

Serious worry crossed Icabod's face. He looked at his feet and tapped his wooden shoes together. "I don't know," he mumbled.

"Did he mention that you might not enjoy working at some flying schools?"

"No," he replied, still looking down.

"That's OK," Henry said, "but these things are important. You don't want to spend all your time and money to find out you don't like the school or instructing, do you?"

"N... no, sir."

I loved how my partner turned things around. He was so positive about it that people rarely noticed. I relaxed.

"I'll tell you what," Henry continued. "We have a written test that determines if you'd like teaching student pilots. If you do and you start training here, we'll consult with you regularly about how it's going and whether you might enjoy working here."

We had no such test. I frowned again.

"What do you think?" he asked Icabod.

The young man looked relieved. "OK," he replied.

My partner stood up. "Good. I'll give you our rate sheet and I'll show you the airplanes you will be flying. They're in the hangar. You can think about it and come back to write the test."

Henry walked over to the flight desk. Icabod stood up and followed him. He seemed relieved to quit the circle of strangers.

Leanne handed my partner a rate sheet from the filing cabinet.

"Here you go," Henry said to Icabod. "Stick this in your pocket so it doesn't get wet. Now let's go to the hangar so you can see our fleet." Henry handed Icabod his raincoat off the peg and opened the door. "I won't be long," he said to us.

Icabod followed him outside like a shadow afraid of losing its body.

Chapter Five

Summer 1, Larry 0

The door closed behind Henry and Icabod. Larry and I looked at each other and burst out laughing. "That kid can't be real," I roared.

"You're right," Larry agreed when he caught his breath. "Icabod, brought to life by a little old wood carver named Geppetto."

"And now Pinocchio is alive and well and looking for work at The Flying Circus," I laughed.

"Hey, you guys, be charitable," Leanne chided from the flight desk. "He's a nice, young man who's a bit shy."

"He's the first pilot I've seen," Larry chuckled, "wearing wooden shoes, flood pants and a raincoat made from inner tubes. He had the worst haircut I have ever seen."

"He was sensibly dressed for the weather," Leanne countered. "If it keeps raining, we'll all need clothes like that."

"Oh sure, Leanne. Can you see me working a Major Airline flight in that uniform?"

"Well, Larry," Leanne replied, "you could finally get your wish."

"What's that?"

"In those shoes, you could walk on water."

Before Larry could respond, the office door opened and Summer McDay bounced in. The cheery young girl flipped back the hood on her yellow rain slicker and shook out her blond ponytail.

"Hi, everyone," she said with a big smile.

Summer was a compact and very fit sports medicine student attending the local university. She helped out as a receptionist on our flight desk some evenings and Saturdays in exchange for flying lessons.

Leanne and I returned her greeting. Larry stood up and dropped into his airline voice.

"Well, if it isn't Summer," he crooned. He walked toward her.

The coed had met the lecherous airline pilot before. "Hi, Larry," she replied, still smiling. She turned and closed the door.

"What brings such a pretty girl out on this nasty day?" he asked.

Summer unzipped her raincoat. Underneath she was wearing a one-piece bathing suit and nothing else. She tilted her head back as the tall pilot stopped close to her.

"I had some time after my pool class this morning," she replied cheerfully. "Since I was already wet, I came out in the rain to see Leanne."

"Well, wet or dry, you're looking good," Larry said, staring at the top of her suit.

"I can see that you're excited," she answered. She pointed at Larry's wet pants. "Is my bathing suit too much?"

Larry looked down at his legs and frowned. "Oh, that. Leanne spilled coffee on me."

"I can see that you're excited." She pointed at Larry's wet pants.

"It looks more like she poured it on you," Summer said.

"She did!"

"Larry, you have to stop treating women like they're second class."

Leanne grinned and nodded in agreement.

"Well, maybe I can start now," Larry purred. "Let me buy you lunch. I know a great restaurant near my place."

"No thanks," she replied. "I'm not dressed for it and neither are you."

"We can go to my house and change first."

"While your wife is at work? I don't think so."

"Hey, better than if she was home."

Henry opened the door behind them. "Hi, Summer," he said.

"Good morning."

"Excuse me folks," Larry said. "I'll be on my way." He gave us a mock salute and left.

Henry looked at me. "Icabod has gone home but I think he'll be back."

"Is that good or bad?" I asked.

"Hey, business is business."

"Who's Icabod?" Summer asked.

Leanne answered. "A nice, young, college graduate interested in becoming a flying instructor."

"Oh, cool."

"Don't get too excited," I said to Summer.

Henry changed the subject. "Leanne, can we afford for me to take you out for lunch?"

"Not really, but I think you should anyway, after I talk to Summer."

He turned toward me. "Would you mind working the desk while I escort our receptionist to lunch?"

I winced. "I'd be happy to except I'm leaving shortly for a ground briefing with Margaret Hathaway at her house." I felt badly. There hadn't been many perks for any of us since starting our business. "How about when I come back?"

"No, it's OK," Henry replied. "We'll stay here. Leanne brought egg sandwiches."

"Leanne's egg beats my bologna on stale bread," I said.

Leanne jumped in. "I can't see Margaret Hathaway having you visit without serving something better than bologna sandwiches."

"I don't think so," I replied. "The lady is in a cast."

"I can cover the desk," Summer offered. "I don't have another class until three o'clock. I'll work in exchange for your egg sandwiches."

"Thanks," Leanne said, "but you don't want to sit here in a wet bathing suit."

Summer blushed a little. "I have warm-up clothes in the car. I took them off for fun when I drove in and saw lecherous Larry's car."

31

Chapter Six

Stuffed

Margaret and Glen Hathaway were a down-to-earth, older couple who had retired with money. They had learned to fly, bought a single-engine Piper Archer and flew it often.

They kept their airplane in The Flying Circus hangar. Henry and I were teaching them instrument flying so they would be less dependent on good weather for their trips.

They had recently returned from Squall Valley, California where Margaret had broken her leg skiing. She had the cast set in a sitting position so she could fly back in the Archer with Glen. She asked if I would teach her instrument ground lessons at home until she was more mobile.

There was a white utility van in the Hathaway's driveway so I parked on the street. Their pink and grey angelstone bungalow was not in the most elite part of the city but the neighbourhood was classy enough that my rusty Volkswagen would temporarily devalue it.

I walked up the driveway and rang the front doorbell. A pleasantly round housekeeper in uniform opened the door and asked me to come in. She took my coat.

"Margaret is expecting you," she said motioning toward the dining room.

Mrs. Hathaway asked everyone to call her, "Margaret".

I took off my wet shoes and walked across the wall-to-wall white shag rug, hoping my two-day-old socks were not leaving dirt marks. My student was seated at an ornate walnut dining table with her ground school kit in front of her. A pair of crutches leaned against the wall behind.

"Hi! Thanks for coming," she said with a smile. "I'm sorry but I won't get up to greet you."

"That's OK," I replied. "You're a trooper just to have this lesson."

Margaret Hathaway could have been "the little old lady from Pasadena." She was grey-haired, medium-height and slim, almost fragile. The dining room furnishings and her clothes were expensive. She looked like someone's aunt waiting for the queen to arrive for tea.

But she wasn't. She was having an instrument briefing with her flying instructor. Her vintage Corvette was tucked in the garage and the airplane sat in the hangar at the airport. When her cast came off, she and Glen would blast off on another adventure.

"Glen is curling at the club," Margaret said. "It's the final bonspiel of the season."

The housekeeper bustled past and into the kitchen.

"You look in good spirits," I said. "Your housekeeper must be taking good care of you."

She blushed. "Oh, I wouldn't have a housekeeper. That's Nan Albert, the caterer. She brought lunch for when you are hungry."

"Ah... OK, I'm not hungry right now," I lied. "Let's learn some instrument flying."

"I'm ready," she smiled.

The caterer reappeared with a tray of glasses filled with different pop and juices. Margaret introduced us.

"I didn't know what you liked to drink," Margaret explained to me, "so I asked Nan to bring a selection. If you prefer something stronger, we can raid Glen's supply."

I took an orange juice. "This is fine, thank you."

Margaret asked for water.

We worked at the table planning a cross-country trip on an instrument chart. Nan Albert bustled out from the kitchen every ten minutes to see if we needed more to drink or something to eat. The smell of simmering soup followed her each time.

It was a difficult lesson for Margaret. Maps used for instrument flying looked naked compared to the visual charts that she had been using. They showed airports, navigation aids and connecting airways but few ground features.

"Glen says that the instrument controllers will guide us on radar so we can't get lost," Margaret mentioned hopefully.

"That's true over built-up areas and at high altitudes but at Piper Archer heights, you'll often be flying without radar coverage."

"Oh, then what?"

"Then you have to know where you are, where you're going, when you'll get there, if you're on track and whether you're clear of the terrain, all without help from ATC."

"Oh."

About an hour later, my stomach growled. At the same time Margaret stifled a yawn.

Nan appeared. "Are you ready for some lunch, Margaret?"

They both looked at me.

"You have to know where you are, where you're going, when you'll get there and if you're on track."

My stomach growled again.

"I guess I am, thank you."

"I have three soups," Nan said, "sweet potato, cream of asparagus or clam chowder."

None of the above, I said to myself. "What are you having, Margaret?" I asked.

"Oh, I'll have a little of your sweet potato, Nan." Then she said to me, "Nan makes wonderful homemade soups. I wasn't sure what you'd like, so there is plenty of everything."

If a cat had been around, I could have asked for clam chowder and shared it but I didn't see one.

"I'll try a little cream of asparagus, thank you," I said.

Nan brought Margaret a bowl half-filled with an orangey broth with parsley flakes sprinkled on top. My bowl was filled to the brim with thick, green cream. It was tasty so I ate it. Margaret sipped three spoonfuls of hers.

Nan also served trays of crackers, breads, cheeses and fruit. Margaret ate two grapes. I had some crackers and a wedge of pumpernickel with cheese.

Then came trays of sandwich quarters and raw vegetables. Margaret took three little bites of a sandwich. I ate several: spicy egg salad, turkey breast with sprouts and shaved roast beef with lettuce and tomato. I was stuffed.

Margaret and I talked about their flight to Squall Valley. More accurately, she talked and I ate.

"Would you like tea or coffee with dessert?" Nan asked me.

"I'm really full," I replied, "but a coffee would be nice, just black, thank you."

She brought tea for Margaret, coffee for me, a serving bowl of trifle and a large tray covered with brownies, butter tarts, custard tarts and raspberry turnovers. They looked homemade.

"I wasn't expecting you to feed me, Margaret." I was pretending to complain. "It was excellent but how can I get an airplane off the ground after eating all this?"

She smiled and scrunched up her nose. "I have two grown sons," she said. "I know young men have hollow legs when it comes to food. Besides, Leanne told me that you are on your own now, so I thought lunch could be a treat."

"It is, thank you, but I can't begin to eat all this."

"Don't worry. Nan will wrap up what we don't finish. You can take it home."

"Oh, you don't have to do that, Margaret," I said, pulling a butter tart from the nearest tray and biting into it. The filling was perfect, thick and moist but not too runny.

I arranged another home lesson with Margaret for the following week. At the insistence of both ladies, I checked off my favourite foods on Nan's catering menu and departed carrying a large, heavy cooler.

"You can return the dishes next week," Nan said. "Don't worry about washing them."

"You're a bachelor's dream," I replied.

Chapter Seven

Leftovers

I carried the caterer's food chest through the rain into The Flying Circus office.

Leanne greeted me from her desk. "Hi. How's our traveling tutor?"

"Stuffed and wet," I replied. I hoisted the cooler onto the nearest table.

"Henry and I were thinking about you slaving away teaching Margaret instrument flying while we ate our friendly little lunch." She held up a small wax paper package. "Summer saved you an egg sandwich."

"Thank you, but I couldn't eat a thing. You were right. Margaret arranged little somethings for my lunch." I flipped the lid up on the chest and tilted it so she could see inside. "The caterer gave me the leftovers. It's more food than I could eat in a week. I thought you could take some home for your monsters."

Leanne and Henry had two pre-teens, a boy and a girl. They ate like locusts on the peak of a seven-year breeding cycle. Leanne got up and walked to the cooler.

"I kept a plate of sandwiches and all of the butter tarts," I grinned. "They're in the car."

"My gosh!" she exclaimed. She lifted the dishes on the top to look underneath. "This would feed an army."

"That's what I thought. We have until my next lesson with Margaret on Tuesday to return the dishes."

"Do you know what this would cost to have catered?" Leanne gasped.

"No, I don't, but when you're figuring it out, add in the price of drinks and a uniformed server."

"Heavens! So while Henry and I were feeling guilty about sharing our skinny lunch special at the restaurant, you were eating from all this?"

I grinned and shrugged. "Someone had to do it. I've already ordered from a menu for our lesson next week."

"I'll go with you," Leanne said quickly. "I'll waitress. It will save Mar-

37

garet the cost of the server."

"I think it was a package deal"

"Too bad," she sighed.

"Where's Henry?" I asked.

"Working in the hangar."

"Give me your keys and I'll carry this out and put it in your car."

"Don't you dare." Leanne grabbed both sides of the cooler. "Go ask Henry to come in for dessert. We're going to eat some of this now before the kids see it."

Chapter Eight

Sex and self-defence

"Summer asked if a couple of girls from her church could use her work credits to start their flying lessons." Leanne was speaking to Henry and me between bites of a raspberry turnover from the cooler.

"What did we tell her?" I asked.

"We said, 'Yes.' She's not using them so I'd rather someone else did than pay her in cash."

"Is Larry going to renew his instructor's rating to teach these girls?" I joked.

Henry smirked. "We're not going to ask him. Larry would be a choir-girl's worst nightmare."

"You never know," I offered. "Larry could be their dreams come true."

"We'll stick to flying lessons," Henry said. "They can learn sex and self-defence somewhere else."

"Chicken," I teased.

"You got that right. We'll get Barry McDay to help us with the extra teaching."

Barry was Summer McDay's older brother. He was an air traffic controller in the Circus Tower. He also had a Commercial Pilot Licence and taught flying for us part time.

"Speaking of teaching," I said, "what was that nonsense about a test for that Icabod guy to find out if he'd like instructing?"

Henry rocked back on the couch and grinned. "Thanks for reminding me," he said. "I have an aptitude test from teacher's college at home. I was going to adapt it to flying to see if Icabod has any instructing bones in his body."

"Henry, the kid can't talk. How could he teach?"

"That's what I'm hoping to find out."

The next person through the door was Barry McDay.

"Hey, I'm glad to see someone is here," he said cheerfully.

"Double congratulations," I added.

"Come in and have some dessert courtesy of Margaret Hathaway," Leanne offered.

"No, thanks, I just had lunch," the slim controller replied. He hung his raincoat on one of the hooks by the door. Barry was an easy-going guy but today he looked more serious than usual. "I dropped by with some news," he said.

"What's up?" I asked.

Barry sat down with us. "You know that Sally and I are expecting another baby."

"Yes," Leanne replied. "How is Sally doing?"

"OK but yesterday the doctor told us that it's twins."

"Wonderful!" Leanne beamed.

"Congratulations," Henry said, reaching over and shaking his hand.

"Double congratulations," I added. "Is it catching?"

Barry laughed. "Not by yourself," he replied.

I looked at Henry. "Maybe you should wash your hands."

"I wanted you to know," Barry said, more seriously, "because Sally needs to take it easy. I won't be flying as much. I want to spend more time helping her with Jennifer."

Henry and I exchanged glances. I shrugged.

"Well, we appreciate all of the work you've done for us, Barry," Henry said. "You're welcome to fly as much as you like."

"Thank you. I'll teach my current students but maybe you shouldn't assign me new ones for a while."

"Sure thing," Leanne replied.

"Well, I gotta go. I'm on the afternoon shift in the tower, although it looks like I won't be very busy in this weather."

"Take a dessert for later," Leanne offered.

"Ah, that's OK," he replied, patting his stomach. "I gotta stay fit."

"Take it from me," Henry said, "your wife won't be making goodies for a long time."

Barry smiled. "You have a point." He helped himself to a custard tart. "Thank you. I'll see you later." He headed out the door.

The three of us looked at each other.

"We're going to have to find another instructor," Henry said.

"Not Icabod!" I exclaimed.

"Do you have someone else in mind?"

I didn't.

Chapter Nine

Idiot proof

"Before I forget," Leanne said to me, "Russ Landsdowne called and asked for you. I left his number beside the phone."

Russ was the insurance agent for The Flying Circus. He was a nice guy and helpful to boot. He had already bailed us out of a couple of situations. I phoned him.

"Hi, Russ. Did you call to see if we're flying in this lousy weather?"

"No," he chuckled. "When you fly is your business. It's only my business if you crash. Then you call me."

"Well, I'm calling but I didn't crash."

"Good. I need a favour."

"Ask me anything. I'll do it."

"This is a big one. You'd better hear me out first."

"Shoot."

"I have a new insurance customer in Derry."

Derry was a large city west of Circus.

"So far, so good."

"He bought a Piper Lance."

The Lance was a big-dollar, high-performance, six-place airplane with a single, 300-horsepower engine, constant-speed propeller and retractable landing gear.

"Nice airplane."

"The owner says he knows you."

This wasn't surprising. I had instructed at the Derry Airport with Henry before we started The Flying Circus.

"What's his name?"

"He speaks highly of you."

"Smart man. Who is he?"

"Edgar Edgar."

I couldn't believe it. Edgar Edgar was an old skinflint pilot who would shut down the engine on the Derry Air rental airplanes when descending to save money on the airtime. I had flown with Edgar during an annual proficiency check. He handled the flying school's simple Cherokee 140s well enough but I couldn't imagine him keeping up to a Piper Lance, let alone paying for one.

"Are you still there?"

"Yes. Are we talking about the same pensioner who flies a Derry Air Cherokee once a month?"

"Probably. He's 88 years old, has a Private Pilot Licence and 292 hours total flying time, 217 as pilot-in-command. He has no experience on high performance aircraft."

"And your request is?"

"Can you check him out on his Lance?"

I answered quickly. "Never in a million years."

"That's what I was afraid of," Russ sighed. "I hate to ask but would you go up with him once just to convince him that it's too much airplane?"

It would be a waste of time, I said to myself, but I hated to refuse Russ. "How about getting Eric Daedalus to fly with him, the chief pilot at Derry Air?"

"I spoke to Eric. He refused. He failed Edgar on his last annual proficiency check. Eric said that Edgar shouldn't be flying anything anymore."

"What happened?"

"Edgar got lost, in the circuit."

"And you think I can check him on an airplane that has twice the horsepower, half again more speed and ten times the systems?"

Russ sighed again. "No, but Edgar trusts you; if you fly with the stubborn old man once, then he'll see that the Lance is more airplane than he can handle."

"Who sold it to him?"

"Buzz Billings."

Billings was the area Piper Aircraft dealer.

"You mean this is a new Lance?"

"Affirmative."

"Holy cow! Edgar must have won a lottery!"

"I don't know where he got the money but he paid cash. Apparently Billings told Edgar that the advanced systems on the Lance were automatic so it was as easy to fly as a Cherokee 140."

"Billings should be shot." I had expressed that opinion on other occasions. The man had a reputation for putting himself first in every deal.

"I agree," Russ said. "The airplane has Piper's new automatic landing gear extension system but I guess that's not enough to save Edgar."

"You've got that right!"

"Edgar's purchase agreement voids the sale if he's unable to pass the insurance check-out."

"Wow! That's not Billings' style. He must have been drunk when he wrote up that one."

"Edgar was smart enough to add the clause himself."

"I'd be happy to send you a letter stating that he can't check out."

"I appreciate what you're saying but it won't work. The purchase agreement requires someone to fly with him before canceling the sale."

I arranged a half-day lesson with Edgar Edgar for the following Monday morning. I did it as a favour to Russ and Edgar. I owed Russ more than one good turn and I had admired old Edgar's spunk when I last checked him out.

A shiny, white and green Lance sat tail low and ready to go on the Derry Airport ramp. I walked up to it. The new airplane was a refreshing sight. The paint was unscratched, the metal was undinged, there were no oil streaks from the engine, no bald spots on the tires and no bugs splattered along the front of the wings. I opened the left rear door and peaked in. The upholstery was unmarred, the carpets were clean and there were no cracks in the plastic trim. I drank in the rich smell of the fresh interior.

There were three rows of paired seats in the long fuselage. The instrument panel was loaded with gauges and radios that I knew Edgar would never use. The tachometer showed a total airtime of 00009.04 hours.

I walked into the flying school. Edgar Edgar was standing at the front counter clutching two fat cushions and shouting at Angel, Derry Air's receptionist. Shouting was the only way Edgar could hear himself.

"As soon as I check out this baby," he hollered, pointing to the Lance, "you and I can take off for Mexico."

The muumuu clad, middle-aged, over-sized spinster nodded agreeably. Angel had never been in an airplane and had no intention of traveling beyond the airport and church but Edgar was a customer. She would let him think whatever he wanted but I knew she would never budge from her stool behind the flight desk.

Eric Daedalus came out of his chief pilot's office behind Edgar. He saw me and shook his head back and forth in sympathy. "Ready for mission impossible?" he asked in a low voice.

Edgar spotted him. "There's that no-good check pilot," he shouted. "This guy couldn't find his own bum with a map!"

"Come on Edgar, you got lost in the circuit," Eric protested.

"I wasn't lost," the older man declared, shaking a gnarled finger at Eric. "I was testing to see if you were." He looked at me. "There you are, sonny. Let's get out of here and bore some holes in the sky." He turned and headed for the door.

I called after him. "I thought we'd have a briefing on the new airplane first."

"Everything is automatic," Edgar declared over his shoulder.

Eric leaned toward me, "Haven't you heard? The Lance is idiot proof. You and Edgar are the perfect test."

I elbowed him in his solid belly.

Across the lounge, the feisty octogenarian had a hand on the door. "Are you here to talk or fly?"

"Both," I replied.

"Then you can talk in the airplane." He opened the door and stepped outside.

"I guess we're flying," I said to Eric and Angel.

Eric grinned. "Do you want my parachute?"

"No thanks."

Angel pulled cotton wads out of her ears. "Do you want these?"

Edgar had learned to fly more than 40 years before in a 65-horsepower Piper Cub, the world's most basic airplane. I knew from experience that he flew Derry Air's Cherokee 140s as if they were Cubs, ignoring improvements such as flaps, instruments, the nosewheel and horsepower. He was too stubborn to change but he made it work. I still didn't know what possessed the little old man to buy such an expensive, sophisticated airplane as the Lance.

Edgar was already perched on his cushions in the pilot seat by the time I reached the Lance.

"How about a pre-flight inspection?" I called through the open door.

"She's new, eh," he answered quickly. "If there's anything not right, she would have crashed on the delivery flight."

"If the engine needed oil," I countered, "Buzz Billings would never pay to have it added."

Edgar knew Billings well enough to understand. He got out and walked around the airplane with me.

"How can I check the oil? I can't reach the dipstick." he grumbled.

He had a point. The oil door was on top of the engine cowling. I had to lift him up by the waist so he could reach it. We repeated the same routine along both wings so he could see the fuel quantity in the four tanks.

"This is embarrassing," he complained. "What do you expect me to do when I'm by myself?"

"Get Angel to come out and goose you," I replied.

That made him smile.

"Do you see that thing sticking out of the side of the fuselage?" Edgar asked, pointing below the pilot's side window.

"Yes."

"This is embarrassing," he complained.

"That's the low-speed sensor for the landing gear," he explained proudly. "It automatically lowers the wheels if the pilot forgets to do it himself. It's idiot proof!"

"Good thing," I replied.

He was obviously repeating Buzz Billings' sales pitch. I thought the feature was funny since Edgar would probably forget to raise the landing gear. I decided since he'd never fly the Lance by himself, I didn't need to spoil his fun, yet. Besides, I wanted to see what happened when he grabbed this tiger by the tail.

The old geezer settled back into the pilot seat. He had one large cushion under him and another behind, ignoring the Lance's six-way adjustable pilot chair. He reached down for his lap belt and accidentally pressed the vertical adjuster. The seat shot upward squishing Edgar's head against the cabin roof.

"What in tarnation?" he exclaimed.

The simple adjusting mechanism was not designed for featherweight fliers. A strong spring pushed the seat up when the pilot took his weight off and pressed the button. The cushion went down when the pilot added his weight and pressed the same button but Edgar wasn't heavy enough.

I reached over and put some weight on his seat. "Hit that button again," I said.

"What button?"

It took a while, but he found it.

"New fangled contraption," he muttered. "The Cub's seat never did that."

"The Cub never did a lot of things," I replied.

"Whad ya say?"

"You're right, Edgar!"

Piper had designed the Lance to be familiar to pilots moving up from the base model Cherokee 140. Edgar soon had the airplane started without using the checklist.

"I'll drive, you talk," he said, pointing to the microphone. He released the parking brake and started the airplane rolling forward.

I turned on the number one communication radio and selected the ground control frequency. I used the old phonetic alphabet so the controllers would know that Edgar was in the airplane. "Derry Ground, this is Lima Able Nancy Charlie Easy, a Lance at Derry Air, taxi for a local flight southeast."

"Lance Alpha November Charlie Echo, Derry Ground, Runway 06, wind calm, altimeter 30.08, taxi Bravo."

"November Charlie Echo," I replied.

I had the receiver turned up for Edgar to hear.

"Is Edgar Edgar flying that airplane?" the controller asked.

"Affirmative. This is a first flight check-out."

Edgar beamed.

"It looks good," the controller responded.

The nosewheel steering on the Lance was heavy. Edgar had to shove hard on the right rudder pedal to turn us onto the runway and then on the left pedal to straighten out. His pushing compressed the cushion behind his back, taking him further from the controls.

"Ready for some real action?" he asked me.

"You're cleared to go," I replied.

Edgar pulled the control wheel back as if he was in a tailwheel airplane. He stretched to see ahead, extended his toes onto the right rudder pedal and applied the 300 horsepower. The engine roared, the Lance charged ahead and commenced a swing to the left.

Torque and gyro effect from the propeller's big paddle blades pulled the airplane to one side. Edgar's leg couldn't reach enough pedal to counteract the swing.

"What the tarnation!" Edgar exclaimed.

The runway was 6,000 feet long and 150 feet wide. I waited to see what the elderly pilot would do.

He yelled at the airplane. "Get over here you stubborn mule!"

The Lance didn't respond.

Then Edgar pulled the power back, reducing the torque. He regained control after some sashaying down the runway.

"Steady, there, Jessibelle!" he called out. He was talking to the horses, all 300 of them.

Edgar reapplied some of the power. He was able to keep the Lance straight, more or less, against the reduced left turning forces but the new Lance was equipped with a "T" tail. The horizontal stabilator sat on the top of the vertical fin above the dirty air swirling back from the propeller. Piper's engineers made the stabilator smaller on the theory that it was more effective up in the clean air. It was, in cruise flight, but not on take-off. The tail's configuration worked against Edgar's out-of-date departure technique.

Piper Cubs didn't have flaps so the stubborn old man had not extended any. He hauled back on the control wheel trying to lever the nose into the air but the smaller stabilator couldn't make it happen. The Lance ploughed along the runway nose high and barely accelerating. The modern, laminar flow wings needed more speed to generate lift. The airplane showed no signs of taking off. In the meantime, Edgar struggled to keep us straight with his toes.

He tried encouragement. "Come on baby, you can do it!"

It didn't work.

I pointed to the diminishing amount of remaining runway. "Time to cut the power, Edgar!"

"Is the airplane still tied down?" he exclaimed.

"No, but I have a few suggestions."

Edgar cut the throttle, slowed the new airplane down and pulled off at the end of the runway. I told the tower controller that we'd be a minute before trying again.

"Roger, do you need the fire trucks yet?" he asked. I could hear a smirk in his voice.

"Negative."

Edgar was frustrated. "This darn mule ain't broke in very well," he declared. "What's wrong with her?"

"Nothing," I replied.

"Well then, it's me or you and I know it's not me! What are you doing wrong?"

I smiled. "You forget that this airplane is automatic. It's designed to take off and climb by itself." It was a lie but it was worth a try.

"You're losing your marbles!"

"Will you try something for me?"

"I'm listening."

I reached below the instrument panel. "See this? It's the rudder trim." I twisted the small wheel a couple of half turns to the right. "There. Now it's set to go straight on the takeoff and climbout. We'll do the same with the pitch trim." I dropped my hand between our seats and pulled on the stabilator adjustment. I pointed to the indicator. "See? Now it's set slightly nose up. Try another takeoff."

"The Cub never had that newfangled stuff."

"That's right. The Cub didn't have all those ponies out front either. You're driving the 300-mule-team Borax wagon now. You have to know some tricks."

Edgar glanced at me sideways. "How do I know you're not jerking my chain?"

"There's one way to find out."

I called the controller. There was no traffic in the circuit. "Derry Tower, Lance November Charlie Echo is ready to take off. Is Runway 24 available?"

"Runway 24 is approved, November Charlie Echo, wind calm. You're cleared for takeoff."

"November Charlie Echo."

Edgar horsed the Lance onto the runway and lined up on the centre-line. He looked at me. I nodded. He gingerly fed in power. The airplane moved straight ahead. Edgar added more power. The Lance accelerated. The pre-set rudder trim kept us in the middle. The old pilot grinned and pushed the throttle lever most of the way. The engine roared, the nose tipped up and the airplane gently lifted into the air.

"Hot diggity!" Edgar whooped.

I dialed the pitch trim down as the nose continued to rotate. Edgar didn't notice.

"Now this is flying!"

We climbed out to the practice area and leveled off at 4,500 feet. Edgar had no trouble with all the systems. He ignored them. He throttled back without touching the propeller governor or mixture controls. I stroked the rudder trim with my foot and the pitch trim with my left hand when needed. He left the landing gear down. Shutting off the back-up electric fuel pump was his only concession to modern aviation.

I offered to show him how to work the radios but Edgar just wanted to fly. He yanked and banked the Lance around, diving and turning to his heart's content. His grin grew wider with each manoeuvre.

"How about testing the automatic landing gear extension system?" I suggested.

Edgar frowned. "What if it doesn't work?"

"Then we lower it manually."

"And if that doesn't work?"

"Then we belly land on the runway and tell Buzz Billings to come and get his faulty airplane."

Edgar liked that. "OK, sonny, on your say so."

I pointed to the gear lever. "First we have to retract it. Pull that knob out and up."

He did. The green, "Gear Down" light went out; the yellow, "Gear in Transition" light came on. There were whirrs from the electric motor and the hydraulic pump under the floorboards. Then the noise stopped and the yellow light extinguished.

"Now what?" Edgar asked.

"Now the wheels are retracted."

He looked out his side and grinned, "Yer right! I can't see them."

"The airspeed is increasing," I said, pointing at the indicator.

"Hot diggity!"

"Try reducing the power and see if the wheels extend on their own."

"Are you sure?"

"Hey, you said it was idiot proof, remember?"

Edgar slowly pulled the throttle back. I rotated the pitch trim wheel to keep the nose from dropping too far.

As the rpm passed below 1700, a cockpit warning horn sounded. "Beep! Beep! Beep! Beep..."

We both jumped in our seats. The Gear in Transition light came on and each of the wheels made a satisfying "thump" as they locked into place. The green light came on and the yellow light went out. The horn continued blaring.

I pointed to the landing gear lever. "Pull it out and down," I shouted.

He did. The horn stopped.

"That sure is idiot proof," Edgar declared.

"Are you ready to head to the airport?" I asked.

"I guess," he replied, adding power.

"OK, raise the landing gear and we'll scoot back."

We both jumped in our seats.

I radioed Derry Tower as we approached the control zone. We were cleared to join the left downwind for Runway 24.

"Edgar, how about doing a pre-landing check?" I asked.

He looked around the cockpit. "All set," he declared. He turned the Lance onto the downwind leg.

"November Charlie Echo is cleared to land Runway 24," the controller said, "wind calm, check gear down."

"November Charlie Echo."

The landing gear was still up. I decided to wait for the "idiot proof" landing gear to lower itself when Edgar throttled back for the landing. I thought the horn might scare him into paying better attention.

"We need the electric fuel pump on," I said.

"Oh, yah."

Edgar reached his right hand across to the row of rocker switches under his side window. He stabbed at the fuel pump. His crooked finger shut off the master electric switch next to it by mistake. He didn't notice.

The master switch controlled all of the electrical systems except the engine ignition. I realized that the automatic landing gear system, the warning lights and the warning horn would no longer work. Edgar was looking outside so he didn't see that the fuel quantity, engine temperature and alternator gauges read zero and that the radios and the electric turn coordinator were dead. The old pilot had found a way to beat Piper's idiot-proof system.

"Edgar!" I shouted. "Is the landing gear down?"

"Just a minute," he replied. He pulled the throttle back. The engine rpm dropped but there was no horn."

"Must be," he declared, "there's no bleeping bleep!" He raised the Lance's long nose to slow down and then turned from a base leg to final. The airplane continued toward the runway with its wheels up.

"Let's overshoot and double check the landing gear," I said. I pointed to the gear selector lever for emphasis. It was in the "up" position.

The elder pilot grabbed the lever and pulled it out and down. Nothing happened.

"There. Are you happy now?"

He continued the approach.

"No, I'm not!" I barked. "Overshoot now!"

"Are you paying for the extra gas?" he countered.

We were less than 200 feet off the ground. The beginning of the runway was sliding under the nose.

I pointed to the darkened "gear safe" green light. "Are you paying for the crash?"

Edgar paused on that piece of information. I placed my hand over his on the throttle lever and shoved it forward.

I was not looking forward to telling Edgar that he would never fly the Lance on his own.

Back on the ground, Edgar parked on the Derry Air ramp and turned the ignition key off to shut down the engine.

"Thanks for flying with me, sonny," he said, turning toward me.

"You're welcome. It was like old times."

"Yes, it was," he said. "That's why I bought the airplane."

"But you're having trouble flying this rocket."

"Oh, for sure!" he answered loudly.

"Why did you buy such a big machine?"

Edgar looked at all the dials and switches in front of us. He smiled. "I wanted to fly once more after Eric told me I couldn't rent their airplanes.

I decided to do it in style."

I waited for him to continue. We sat there listening to the gyro instruments spinning down.

"There had to be an easier way to fly in style than buying a Lance," I suggested.

"Easier, maybe, but this has been a lot of fun. I got to scare the heck out of the bank by withdrawing all my money. I had Buzz Billings, my dimwit, ex-son-in-law, dancing on a string to sell me this brand new aircraft. For one day at the airport, I was more than just a loud, old, skinflint rental pilot. I got to fly a high performance airplane for free. And next, I get to see the look on Billings' stupid face when I'm returning the airplane. That's pretty good entertainment for an old guy from a retirement home."

Chapter Ten

Surprise

Snappy Shuttlecock telephoned on the next bad weather day. It had been a couple of weeks since I had splashed him with Lake Erie. I recognized his noseless, whistling voice right away.

"Oh, you're there!"

"Yes, sir," I replied.

He hung up.

"Nice talking to you..."

"Who was that?" Leanne asked.

"It was Shuttlecock, the tyrant photographer," I replied. "I think he's on his way over, but I don't know why. I thought we'd never hear from him after I dipped the Cub tire in the lake. He didn't sound happy."

Leanne smiled, "He never sounds happy."

"He probably wants his money back."

"Oh, I don't think so. Guys like him try to be gruff but their bark is worse than their bite."

Snappy burst through the office door and stumbled to a stop a few feet into the room. He whipped out a large envelope from under his wet trench coat and plopped it on the nearest table.

"Gather around. I have something to show you," he announced with a flourish.

Leanne, Henry and I were sitting at different places in the office doing paperwork. Leanne got up and closed the front door. Henry and I joined Snappy.

The lopsided photographer pulled a handful of photo proofs from the package. "You missed this shot altogether!" he declared, slapping down the first picture.

It was an overhead shot of the Harry Bottom III. The ship was moving well out of the sun's reflection on the lake.

"And you're too high in this one."

He dropped a side-view photo on top of the first. The ship's hull glowed black in the sunlight but everything above blended into the watery background.

Next was a similar shot taken a little lower. The ship's deck was in line with the hazy horizon making it look like it was attached there. "Still too high," Snappy declared.

He continued to criticize several other pictures as if I had taken them. At the last one he said, "And this is too low!"

It must have been taken as the Super Cub's tire touched the lake. The ship was mostly obliterated by water splashing up in front of the lens.

Snappy looked at Henry and Leanne. "Your pilot was trying to give me a bath!"

I thought I detected a slight smile in his voice but his deformed face didn't show it, or couldn't.

Henry turned to me, "Now I believe you."

"You believe what?" the photographer asked.

"I thought my partner was pulling my leg about hitting the water."

"Well, I thought it was the end of a very expensive camera," Snappy said.

"And airplane," Henry added.

"And customer," Leanne said.

I just shrugged and grinned.

"I have one more picture in the Rover to show you but I need a hand bringing it in." He looked at Henry as he spoke.

"Sure," my partner replied. He grabbed his raincoat off the peg and followed Snappy out the door.

"So, does he want his money back?" I asked Leanne.

"No, I think he's showing you how to position the airplane better for next time."

"Why do you look for the good side of everything?"

She smiled. "Because I always find it."

Snappy shoved the door open and struggled into the room carrying the front of a plywood-sized board. It was draped in a dark plastic tarp. Henry was on the other end. Leanne went over and closed the door behind them.

They negotiated the load around the briefing tables and chairs to the wall opposite the windows. They set the bottom edge on the floor.

"Now lift the wrap off," Snappy said to Henry.

They pulled up the covering. I stepped forward to help. The photographer shooed me away saying, "Go stand by the windows."

Underneath the covering were two blank sheets of four by eight-foot plywood. They laid the tarp on the floor and then lifted the sheets, setting the bottom edges across two tables. They leaned the tops against the wall.

"Your pilot was trying to give me a bath!"

"Now hold onto the edges," Snappy said to Henry, "while I walk this side of the front one around. They go end-to-end."

I watched from across the room as a four-foot high by 16-foot long image of the Harry Bottom III was assembled in front of me. It was the stern quarter shot that Snappy had taken just before we touched the lake. The ship's aft superstructure loomed large on the right. The name appeared across the round stern above the white water boiling out from the propeller in the foreground. The long image tapered off toward the bow as it headed to the horizon. The picture was magnificent. It was taken from below the deck level. The scrawny, misshapened photographer had captured the size and power of the huge vessel perfectly.

Snappy held up both arms toward the huge photo and announced triumphantly, "This shot is just right!" His face contorted in an attempted smile. "This will be mounted in the boardroom at the shipping company headquarters," he said. "I thought you'd like to see it first."

We were speechless.

"What do you think?" Snappy whistled.

"The detail is wonderful," Henry finally said. "I can see the individual flags and halyards on the signal mast above the bridge."

"That's the beauty of shooting with the Hasselblad from an airplane: large lens, plate format and close range."

The man seemed happy about the photo but it was hard to be sure. I didn't say anything.

He turned to me. "Next week we fly to Collingwood to shoot a new ship running on its acceptance trials. Book me Tuesday for the whole day leaving at eight o'clock."

Chapter Eleven

Pheasant Island

A cold front cleared out the early summer smog the night before Snappy and I went hunting for another ship. We departed early on a crisp, cool day in the Super Cub and flew toward lower Georgian Bay.

We bounced along in a headwind all the way. Our groundspeed averaged 70 mph. Snappy grew antsy. He was paying by the hour and the slow pace bugged him.

Comfort was not part of the Super Cub's design. The back seat in the grass roots airplane was cramped. Cool drafts whistled in through the poorly fitted windows and door. I could feel Snappy constantly shifting around behind me, fussing with his equipment and trying to keep warm. He had dressed in his winter fatigues but not much heat got past the pilot. There was little padding in the plywood seats and no cabin service. It took us two slow hours to fly to the Collingwood Airport where we landed to refuel.

My passenger told me that our photo target was registered as the "Dividend". This followed the Lake Land Shipping's tradition of naming new freighters after balance sheet optimism. Snappy had chosen today for the trip because the ship was scheduled for trial runs at full speed while loaded down with water ballast.

We had a few minutes to stretch and warm up on the ground at Collingwood. Snappy didn't say much. He was obviously anxious to find the ship. He was already strapped back into the airplane when I returned from paying for the fuel.

I spotted the new freighter from 20 miles away. It was an impressive sight, gleaming in the sunshine, charging proudly into the wind and waves northwest bound from Collingwood. She was riding low, churning up white water at her stern and trailing a large wake.

"There she blows!" I announced.

Snappy unfastened his seat belt, leaned forward and looked over my shoulder. The scene made him forget to be sullen.

"Yes! This is perfect!" he whooped. "Give them a quick recognition pass and then we'll get to work." He sat back and gathered up his equipment.

I could have told him that the ship was still 15 minutes away but I didn't want to dampen his new-found enthusiasm.

As we drew closer, I could see that the Dividend's crew was expecting us. Signal flags had been run up and the decks were clear of gawkers.

The ship was a monster. All of the superstructure was built aft. An endless row of hatch covers marched from the bridge to the bow.

I flew parallel to the port side and gave the Cub's wings a friendly rock. I could see faces in the side windows of the bridge. Snappy had said that the control room would be crowded with acceptance engineers from the shipyard and the government transport department plus the crew and possibly some investors. I waved to them. They waved back.

Snappy had been told that the captain would not deviate from his course during the trials. Our plan was to photograph the port side with the sun behind us and then wait for the Dividend to turn around for her run back to the shipyard. Then we could shoot with the sun on the starboard side.

"Set up for a pass like this but lower and closer in," Snappy said over the intercom. "I'm ready for the door when you are," he added.

I flew straight on, reduced the power, raised the nose, lowered the flaps and trimmed for 65 mph. I switched the aircraft radio to the emergency frequency as a precaution, checked the airplane's systems and then opened the split door.

I banked to the left and descended. By the time I had turned a complete circle, the wind had carried us behind the ship. It looked like we were barely moving. Our ground speed into the wind would have been about 45 mph. The ship was steaming at 15 mph giving us a closing rate of 30.

Out of the corner of my eye, I could see Snappy lean into the slipstream holding onto his big aerial camera. I lifted the right wing, pushed the right rudder pedal to hold us in a forward slip. I added power to hold us off the water. Snappy snapped and slapped away with the shutter and plates.

"Closer in!" he yelled over the wind noise.

I pushed more right rudder. The Cub curved in toward the stern quarter. The ship grew in size while our view barely moved forward.

"Good, good! Keep it coming. Perfect!"

Snappy grabbed more plates from the case behind him. "Can you slide away like you slid in?"

"Yes, sir."

I relaxed slightly on the rudder. The Cub slipped sideways away from the ship while our view inched forward.

"Can you drop down while sliding away?" he asked. I could see Snappy out of the corner of my eye looking at the lake's surface as he spoke.

"Yes, sir. No problem."

The Dividend was so huge that I didn't have to touch the water's surface for Snappy to shoot up at it. He didn't have to lean out as far either. We pulled even with the stern.

"This is excellent!" he exclaimed. "Now climb slowly while holding this distance."

I added power. The next sequence would have made a great IMAX movie. Our view of the long black hull and the white superstructure dropped away to include the bright red deck and the sky beyond as the Cub gained height.

"Keep going up and move over the ship!"

I did.

Snappy snapped and slapped some more. He stopped as we were approaching amidships and gave me a twisted grin. "This is like shooting fish in a barrel!"

He looked at the ship and then moved his hand like an airplane. "Now, can we bank away from her while descending?"

"Yes, sir!"

"And can you lift the wing more?"

"I can," I replied, "but it will bring the propeller into your view."

"That's OK."

The photographer turned, leaned out further and pointed the Hasselblad behind the strut. This was a new one on me. Three quarters of his body was outside of the airplane.

I quickly reduced the power, switched hands on the stick, added left bank and reached for the back of his pants. The right wing came up and the Cub slid away from the ship, descending toward the surface of the lake. Snappy's final frames were shot to the rear and upward with the bow looming in the foreground and the rest of the giant ship tapering away.

Snappy flopped back into his seat. "That's it!" he declared. "That one slow pass gave me all the shots I need from this side." He checked his watch. "It will be at least an hour before she turns around."

I banked us away from the ship. Orbiting for an hour seemed like a waste but it would have taken an hour to fly to the Collingwood Airport and back. I looked around. There was a round-shaped, 300-acre island between the shore and us. It was covered with trees except for an east-west slash in the bush across the south end. I flew toward it.

There was a small lodge with outbuildings on the south shore. The opening in the trees nearby was a grass landing strip. I pointed to it.

Three quarters of his body was outside of the airplane.

"We could land there to stretch our legs and wait," I said. I knew that saving airtime charges would appeal to my passenger.

"Sure, if you think it's OK."

"There's one way to find out."

I circled and lined up for a westerly low pass to inspect the strip. From 200 feet up, it looked well maintained. I estimated it to be at least 2,500 feet long with clear approaches over the shorelines at both ends. It was open except for a few large birds dotting the runway.

"It looks good," I called out. "Seat belt on?"

"I'm in."

I swung the airplane around in a tight, left-hand circuit and set up for a precautionary landing into the wind. The flaps were already down. I flew a slow approach, touched at the beginning of the grass strip and stopped short. The nearest birds scattered indignantly but did not fly away. I taxied over to a small parking area off the runway and shut down.

We unfolded ourselves from the Cub, stretched our limbs and looked around.

"It's like a movie set," Snappy said.

I could see what he meant. The trees in the surrounding bush had been trimmed of their branches from the ground up to five feet. By ducking down, I could see quite a distance.

"Robin Hood and his merry men should come riding out of the forest any time," I said.

"He won't get much robbing me," Snappy replied.

The birds on the runway were pheasants. They kept their distance while pecking in the grass.

There were wire baskets with lids hung on a few tree trunks. I pointed to one. "What do you make of those?"

"I think we've landed at a rich men's hunting camp," Snappy replied.

The silence was broken by the sound of a vehicle coming from the direction of the buildings to the south. A black Chevrolet Suburban appeared through the trees along a rutted track and stopped not far from us. An emblem on the door read, "Pheasant Island Hunting Club".

A short, stocky man climbed out of the driver's side wearing a safari-type green uniform and a frown.

"What are you doing here?" he asked with forced authority.

Snappy beat me to a reply. "Hello there. We are from the Federal Transport Department, Marine Division," he said. "My name is Cameron Shuttlecock and this is my pilot." His tone was friendly but firm.

I nodded.

Snappy pointed to the Dividend still visible in the distance beyond the end of the runway. "We're shooting photos of that new ship during its acceptance trials. We just landed to stretch our legs and wait for it to reverse course."

The man stared at Snappy's rearranged face. He tried to hide his curiosity but failed. He looked at the ship and then me. "This is a private island," he said. "It's for the exclusive use of club members." The words sounded rehearsed. He was being a loyal employee.

"Oh, we're dreadfully sorry," Snappy replied. "We didn't know. We weren't planning to stay long."

"Well, if you take off as soon as you have stretched your legs, I guess it'll be OK, but stay with your airplane. We have important club members and their guests eating lunch in the lodge."

"That's very kind of you," Snappy said. "We won't cause you any trouble." He looked around. "Tell me. What do your members hunt here?"

"Pheasants," the man replied.

I looked along the airstrip. It must be tough to do, I thought to myself. I could have bagged two or three birds with the airplane during the landing.

"I see," Snappy said. "And you trim the trees so the hunters can have a clear shot?"

"Actually, the deer do the trimming," our greeter replied. Snappy's friendly approach seemed to be thawing his sternness. "We're overrun with white tails. They come across on the winter ice and get marooned here."

"Can't you shoot the deer?"

"No. The pheasants are raised here at the lodge so they're ours to harvest, but the deer are wild. They fall under the same game laws as the rest of the area."

"Interesting," Snappy said.

"Well, I'll get back to work at the lodge," the guy said. "Stay as long as you need," he added. "Just don't wander around."

"Yes, of course. Thank you very much," Snappy replied.

The man climbed into the truck, turned it around and drove back toward the buildings.

Snappy squatted on his haunches and watched the ship disappear behind the trees on the north side of the landing strip.

I fetched a lunch bag and thermos from under my seat in the Super Cub and sat down on the grass beside my passenger.

"Would you like a sandwich?" I asked. I pulled out several kinds of catered leftovers and placed them on the bag. They were days old but I had kept them in the fridge at home and they hadn't killed me yet. "There's chicken, salmon and egg salad."

Snappy seemed surprised by my generosity. "Are you sure?"

"Yes. I brought extras for you, unless you have something better for us in your camera bag."

"Only if you like to eat dead batteries and cleaning fluid," he said.

Snappy's face blushed various shades of blotchy pink and red.

"Only if you like to eat dead batteries and cleaning fluid," he said. His dappled skin twisted as he tried to grin.

"No, thanks," I replied. It was the first time I had seen him relax enough to show some humour. I wondered how the man could change from difficult to friendly so quickly.

"Help yourself," I said, moving the bag closer to him.

"Thank you." He took a sandwich. "Bachelors like me don't get good food often. Did your wife make these?"

"No, no wife," I answered. "I'm tutoring an older lady in her home. She provides a catered lunch during the lesson. These are some of the left-overs."

"You're kidding! What are you teaching her?"

"Flying. I'm prepping her for the instrument flying exam."

Snappy shook his head back and forth. "I'm in the wrong business." He bit into the sandwich.

I grinned. "Cushy, eh?"

He nodded in agreement. We munched in silence for a few moments.

"I guess I don't measure up to your other customers," Snappy remarked. "I don't have our flights catered."

"Well, I appreciated the way you handled Mr. Hunting Club just now."

"That was easy. A little friendliness and respect go a long way."

"Leanne has been trying to teach me that," I said.

Snappy focused his good eye on me and frowned. "You're telling me that I should have shown your receptionist more friendliness and respect?"

Oops! I hadn't been thinking about how he had ignored Leanne when he first came to our office but the comparison fit. I scrambled for a reply. "She could be your best friend if you did," I offered.

"I get so tired of bad reactions when I meet people, especially women, that I go on the offensive." He sounded more defeated than bitter.

I took a chance. "It didn't work on Leanne, did it?" I smiled to show that I meant no malice.

"Ha!" Snappy laughed. "That's for sure! I lost that round fair and square." His laughter was like his speech. Half of it whistled out his stub of a nose but it sounded genuine. "She had my number that day!"

It was my turn to nod in agreement. I filled the thermos cap. "Some lukewarm coffee?" I offered. "It's black."

"Thank you." He took a sip.

"Do you talk about your injuries?" I asked quietly.

He looked at me again. This time there was no frown. "Not often," he replied. "They're not injuries. I was born like this. Every operation since has made it worse."

65

I felt sorry for him but I figured he didn't need to know that. "Then you've been seeing bad reactions for a long time."

He nodded.

We ate more lunch and shared the rest of the coffee. I wasn't sure what else to say. "How did you get into photography?" I asked.

His face twisted in an attempted grin. "It's a job where I can hide my good looks behind a camera and work with my one good eye."

"You have a talent for it," I said. "That picture you brought into the office was fantastic."

"Thank you," he said. He pointed to where the ship had disappeared. "I wanted to be a sea captain but I couldn't make the binoculars work."

I looked to see if he was being serious. He started to laugh. So did I.

"Do you think I could guide one of those monsters through a canal?" he chuckled. He rolled his eyes around in different directions.

"I don't know. If ship captains do it drunk, I bet you could do it sober."

We both laughed some more.

The humour transformed Snappy's deranged face from scary to merry. When laughing, he looked like a clown, a happy one who used a lot of make-up to appear comical. His camouflage clothing made a good costume to complete the picture.

"It's good to see you laugh," I said.

"Thanks for being an accomplice," he replied. "It's been a while."

I looked around and changed the subject. "So these big game hunters shoot the birds," I speculated out loud, "and drop them into the baskets on the trees. Then Mr. Uniform gathers them and the kitchen staff clean and cook them to serve for lunch in the lodge."

"Sounds about right," Snappy replied.

"Great sport!" I said.

"Not if you're a pheasant," he chuckled.

Chapter Twelve

Medevac

Snappy and I were interrupted by the return of the truck. It charged out of the bush in a big hurry and jerked to a halt next to us. The driver in the safari suit jumped out looking frightened. I could see other people in the truck. Snappy and I stood up.

"We need your help!" the driver shouted.

Other doors on the Suburban burst open. Three older men stumbled out. One was doubled over.

"George needs a hospital!" the driver declared. "Can you fly him?"

The other men looked old and rich. They were dressed in expensive, new, hunting garb. The one was obviously in pain. He moaned loudly between coughing and heaving. A buddy was holding him so he couldn't fall over.

The fourth man looked at the Super Cub, frowned, and then turned toward Snappy and me. His frown deepened when he saw Snappy's face. He spoke to me.

"We don't know what's wrong with George," he said. He spoke quickly and with a deep, authoritative voice. "He just collapsed during lunch. We radiotelephoned for an emergency airlift but it will take two hours for a helicopter ambulance to get here from Toronto." He glanced at the Super Cub. "We thought you had a real airplane but this will have to do. Fly George to Toronto and he'll get there a lot sooner."

Several thoughts flooded my head. It would take me an hour and a half to fly to Toronto. During that time I could do nothing for George's care or comfort. If he was going to die, I'd rather he didn't do it crammed into the back of the Super Cub. A helicopter could land right at a hospital. I couldn't. If I did the trip, Snappy would miss shooting the ship's starboard side. No matter what decision I made, the outcome would be my responsibility.

I looked at Snappy. He was looking at me. He turned to the man of authority and said, "If my pilot agrees, he can fly your friend to the

Collingwood Airport. He would be in the care of ambulance attendants within 30 minutes and on his way to the local hospital."

The suggestion made more sense to me.

The older man turned to Snappy, "I wasn't asking!" he barked. He stepped closer to me and boomed in my face, "Toronto has the best doctors and facilities. Get George in that aircraft and take him there, now!"

I looked at Snappy again. He made a hand gesture that the man did not see. He was pointing toward Collingwood.

"Yes sir!" I replied smartly. "You and your buddies load George into the airplane and strap him in. Then go back to the lodge and cancel the air ambulance. I'll arrange to be met at the airport on my way there."

I climbed into the Super Cub, buckled up and started flipping switches. Snappy helped George's buddy walk the sick man to the airplane. They turned him around and leaned him into the door opening. George was rotund. There was not enough room behind the wing strut for more than one helper. Snappy pushed the other man out of the way, shoved his hands under George's armpits and horsed his torso into the back seat with surprising strength. George screamed in pain and then puked on himself and Snappy. The photographer ignored it and lifted George's legs in behind my seat. He reached in and dug out the passenger seat belt. I punched the starter button. Snappy put his face near my ear and whistled one word, "Collingwood?"

I nodded in reply. He stepped back. I looked ahead and added throttle. The Cub moved forward. I turned onto the runway, checked the airplane's systems, closed the door and looked at George. He was rocking and moaning.

"Hang in there buddy!" I yelled and applied full power.

I took off from beside the parking area and turned enroute as soon as I was above the treetops. I headed for Collingwood climbing to 3,500 feet. Once there, I leveled off and radioed for an ambulance.

"Collingwood Unicom, this is Super Cub Charlie Uniform Bravo, a medevac 40 miles northwest at 3,500 inbound for landing. Request an ambulance to rush one patient from the airport to the Collingwood hospital."

Several moments passed before I received a hurried reply. "Medevac inbound Collingwood, I have ambulance dispatch on the line. State patient details and your estimated time of arrival, over."

"The medevac is Super Cub Charlie Uniform Bravo, estimate Collingwood in 20 minutes. I have one 70-year-old male doubled over in pain."

A few moments later the unicom operator at Collingwood said, "Charlie Uniform Bravo, the ambulance is on its way. State your last point of departure."

"Uniform Bravo is out of Pheasant Island. I'm 30 miles northwest, request your airport advisory."

"Charlie Uniform Bravo, Collingwood active runway is 31, wind northwest at 20, altimeter 30.11, no reported traffic."

"Uniform Bravo."

I spotted the Collingwood Airport well back. I descended with the power on and flew straight into the left downwind leg of Runway 31. I could see the ambulance with its lights flashing turning onto the airport entrance road. I kept my pattern in tight and landed well down the runway, close to the turn-off at the end.

I parked the Cub near the waiting ambulance and shut down the engine. I turned and looked at George. He had stopped rocking and moaning. His eyes were open and red. He belched loudly and looked around.

He asked me questions about the patient that I couldn't answer.

"Wherrre ammm IIII?" he groaned. He sounded drunk.

I opened the Cub's door and hopped to the ground. Then I reached in and unfastened George's seatbelt. His hunting vest was covered in barf and he had wet his pants.

Two paramedics approached with a gurney on wheels. "What do we have here?" one asked.

"I don't really know," I replied, getting out of their way. "His name is George and he doubled over in pain during lunch."

One medic checked George while the other scribbled notes on a clipboard. He asked me questions about the patient that I couldn't answer.

"Call the Pheasant Island Hunting Club," I suggested. "They'll know about him. I don't have the number."

"OK, we'll take him from here," clipboard said.

They eased him out of the airplane, onto the gurney and into the ambulance. The siren and lights came on. They roared away.

I was left standing beside an empty airplane on an empty ramp. My emotions were mixed. My body was still high on adrenaline from the rushed flight. It felt good to have helped. I suspected that George would recover as soon as excess booze and pheasant were pumped out of his stomach. I was anxious to finish the photo shoot with Snappy but I wasn't looking forward to facing his buddies after ignoring their "orders".

I turned toward the nearest airport building. Four people were watching me through a window. I headed that way to arrange for more fuel, to wash George's puke off my hands and to get a cloth to clean the urine off the Cub's seat.

The first person inside the building stopped me cold. It was Inspector Kennedy, a crusty, old, government aviation inspector. Over the last ten years, Kennedy and I had developed lowering opinions of each other during several unhappy encounters. Now he was standing in my way in his signature rumpled dark suit with his granite face frowning and his hands on his hips.

"I see you are flying medical evacuations now." He said it like he was reading a death sentence.

I knew that any reply could and would be used against me. The Flying Circus was not licenced to fly medevacs.

"Good afternoon, sir," I said.

He reached inside his suit coat and withdrew a notebook. He scribbled in it for a moment. "We will see about this," he said. Then he turned and walked toward two people seated nearby.

"Nice talking to you, sir," I mumbled, low enough so he couldn't hear.

I took my time flying back to Pheasant Island. I didn't have a choice.

The wind was on the nose and still strong. I set up for a straight-in approach to the landing strip. On my right, I could see the Dividend steaming southwest for home. There was still time for Snappy and me to photograph her starboard side.

I touched down on the beginning of the grass and swung into the parking area in one curving motion. Snappy was sitting alone under a tree nearby. He got up as I shut down the engine.

I opened the Cub's door and called to him. "I see the members of the Pheasant Island Hunting Club invited you to their lodge to wine and dine in a warm showing of appreciation."

"Not that bunch!" Snappy replied. He brushed the pine needles off the back of his fatigues. "How did you make out?"

"According to plan," I replied. "George is in the Collingwood General Hospital and recovering by now. I suspect he was suffering from acute indigestion and maybe alcohol poisoning."

I sat in the pilot's seat while Snappy walked up to the airplane.

"It figures," he said.

"Thanks for your help on that one," I added.

"I didn't do much."

"What you did, worked. Now do you want to roll out of here before they come out of the lodge or stay and tell them what I didn't do?"

"Departing is tempting," Snappy said with a twisted face for a grin, "but we'd be acting too much like them."

The sound of the Suburban charging through the bush took away thoughts of skipping out.

"Too late," I said, climbing out of the Cub.

The black truck stopped at the edge of the clearing. The larger, older man swung down from the right front seat. George's other buddy got out from behind him. They marched toward me. The uniformed staff member stayed in the cab.

"So, is George in the hospital?" Mr. Authority demanded to know. "What's happening?"

I decided not to antagonize them more than necessary. "I left George in the care of the ambulance medics," I replied. "He was awake and talking when I last saw him." I didn't mention that George was asking who puked on his hunting jacket and why were his pants wet.

"That's our George," the man said approvingly. He nodded to his buddy and then turned back to me. "Which hospital did they take him to?"

It occurred to me that this important person had not figured out that I had returned too soon. I should have been just touching down in Toronto as we spoke.

"The General," I replied.

71

"Good. I know several excellent doctors there," Mr. Authority declared. "Did you get a phone number for us to call and check on him?"

"No, sir, I did not."

"Figures! Well, we'll find it." He turned to his friend, "Come on, we can use the radiophone in the lodge." He started walking toward the truck.

Snappy spoke up. "Excuse me, sir!"

Mr. Important turned and looked down his nose toward the photographer. "What?"

"Could we have a contact to send an invoice for the flight?"

The guy's face wrinkled into a serious frown. "I thought you worked for the government?" he barked.

This is where Snappy gets caught in a lie, I thought.

"The pilot works for an air service which I have contracted," Snappy replied, just as loudly.

"Then put the flight in your contract and tell your government to take it out of my taxes!" the big man roared. He placed one hand on the open door and a foot on the running board.

"I can't do that, sir," Snappy replied. At the same time, he lifted a 35mm camera to his good eye and triggered the shutter.

The man shook a finger at Snappy. "If I hear anything from you, Scarface," he bellowed, "you'll be in big trouble!"

He motioned for the driver to go back to the lodge. They had to wait. The other club member was still waddling toward the truck. The driver's window was open. I walked toward it. George's other buddy yanked open the door behind the driver and hauled himself in. The driver rammed the Suburban into reverse. Just before he stepped on the gas, I called out, "George is in the Collingwood General!"

Chapter Thirteen

The test

"Where's Henry?" I asked Leanne as I came through the office door.
"Flying with Icabod Brimsmead," she replied.
"Pinocchio?"
Leanne's voice dropped into schoolteacher mode. "Don't call him that. It'll stick."
"Do you think Icabod is a better name than Pinocchio?"
"It's his name," she frowned. "Anyway, he came in, took Henry's test, did well and signed up for the instructor's course. Henry was available for a lesson so they're flying now."
"I don't believe it."
"Which part: that Icabod came back, that he did well on the test or that he started the course?"
"Yes," I replied.
Leanne pulled a single sheet from a file and dropped it on the flight desk. "Have a look," she said. "Icabod scored 90 per cent."
The page was a copy of Henry's exam.

Instructor Candidate Test

Choose one answer for each question:

1/ When did you decide to become a flying instructor?
a) This year b) Age 20 and up c) Before age 20

2/ How many model airplanes did you build while growing up?
a) 0 b) 1-9 c) 10 or more

3/ How many model airplanes did you help other kids build?
a) 0 b) 1-4 c) 5 or more

4/ Which was your favourite movie?
a) Top Gun b) Memphis Bell c) To Sir, With Love

5/ If you were allowed to visit an airline cockpit in flight, you would:
a) Want to fly the plane
b) Want to watch the plane being flown
c) Want to ask the pilots how to fly the plane

6/ After you purchase something, the first thing you want to do is:
a) Try it out b) read the instructions c) show someone how it works

7/ How many organizations have you volunteered to teach for in your lifetime? (Examples: Sunday school, scouts, guides, cadets, etc.)
a) 0 b) 1-4 c) 5 or more

8/ How often have you referred to an aviation textbook in the last month?
a) 0 b) 1-4 c) 5 or more

9/ How many speeding tickets have your received in the last year?
a) 5 or more b) 1-4 c) 0

10/ What minimum annual salary would you accept as a full-time flying instructor?
a) $25,000 b) $20,000 c) $15,000

"If Icabod scored 90 per cent, then the correct answer is always 'c'," I said.
"That's right. You go to the head of the class."
"I wouldn't if I had taken this test. It's rigged!"
"Sure it is. It's rigged to show teacher potential."
"So which question did Icabod miss?"
"The movie question. He had not seen any of them."

Chapter Fourteen

Hop-a-long Hathaway

"Margaret Hathaway booked a flying lesson with you for this evening at seven o'clock," Leanne said to me.

"So soon? She was just getting her cast off at the beginning of this week."

"She said she missed flying and wanted to do a few circuits."

"Good. She's more fun when I'm not trying to teach her something."

I watched Margaret hobble from her Corvette to the office. She was wearing leather pumps, pastel slacks and a white blouse under a fringed, colourful shawl. A dangling necklace and matching dangling earrings completed what would be her generation's most casual look.

The slim, older lady was trying to use a cane. Each time she placed weight on her bad left leg, she lurched left and launched her right arm into the air, like a rodeo rider maintaining balance. Then she stabbed the sidewalk with the cane as an afterthought.

I opened the office door.

"The doctor told me that I'd be sorry if I tried to do too much," she said without looking up. "I guess he was right but I didn't want to be housebound any longer."

"Well, if it isn't Hop-a-Long Hathaway," I teased. "Come on in."

Margaret stopped at the two steps leading into the office. She was not sure which combination of good leg, bad leg, hands or cane to use. "Now don't make fun of a weak, little, old lady."

I helped her up. "You're doing fine," I lied, "but I think you should stay out of china shops for a while."

Summer was working the flight desk so I left Margaret to rest her leg and exercise her lips while I pulled her airplane out of the hangar and checked it over.

"So, we'll do some circuits to get you flying again?" I asked when I returned.

"Yes, please," she replied. "I love flying at sunset. I've been looking forward to this all day."

Margaret might have been feeble at walking but not at flying. To get into her low-wing Piper Archer, she sat on the right side trailing edge of the wing and bum-slid backward up hill on the gritted catwalk to the door. Then she hand-walked backward across the cockpit and plopped into the left seat.

I climbed in beside her. Margaret then spent a few minutes adjusting her seat, whisking her fingers through her hair, wiping her nose with a tissue, checking her lipstick in the sunvisor and pulling a bag of candy from the depths of her purse.

"English mint?" she offered.

"Yes, thank you," I replied. I had nothing else to do so I took two.

The sun was just setting when Margaret retrieved the checklist from a sidewall pocket. She shifted into high gear. Her hands pranced over the switches and controls. She had the engine started in no time. She turned the radio on and asked for taxi instructions for practice touch and goes.

"Mike Victor Golf Hotel, Circus Ground, Runway 24, wind 250 five to ten, altimeter 30.11, cleared to taxi Charlie, Delta, Bravo."

"Mike Victor Golf Hotel, roger, thank you."

She released the parking brake and started taxiing toward the runway.

"Welcome back, Mrs. Hathaway," the controller added.

Margaret wrinkled her nose happily. "Why thank you," she transmitted. "Is this John?"

"Yes it is, Mrs. Hathaway. It's good to hear you on the frequency."

"Why thank you, John, but please call me Margaret."

Margaret knew all of the local air traffic controllers by name. She visited the tower often, always carrying desserts for her "boys". None of them called her Margaret, probably because she dressed, talked and acted like everyone's great aunt.

She didn't fly like a great aunt.

We were parked beside the runway by the time she finished exchanging pleasantries with John. She completed a quick pre-take-off check and changed the frequency to Circus Tower. I was watching her. So far she had not missed anything.

"Mike Victor Golf Hotel, ready for takeoff Runway 24 for the circuit," she said into her boom mic.

It was the same controller working both positions. "Victor Golf Hotel is cleared for takeoff Runway 24, wind 240 at five to ten, call downwind."

Margaret started the Archer rolling onto the runway. "Thank you, John." She wrinkled her nose at me again. "I mean, Victor Golf Hotel, roger."

She applied full throttle.

The top of a big orange sun was just disappearing below the horizon in the pink sky to our right.

"Don't you love flying in the evening?" Margaret asked over the full power engine noise.

"I like flying anytime," I replied, "but pink skies are special times for lady pilots."

She gave me a quick smile. "Ahh, that's so sweet!"

By now, the Archer had enough airspeed to lift off. Margaret eased it into the air and then held the nose down. We accelerated just above the centreline of the runway.

I was not concerned about Margaret's odd way of departing. She always did this when she was not carrying passengers, other than me. I clamped my mint between my teeth and braced myself for what was coming next.

The airspeed indicator was well over 100 mph when the little old lady from Circus hauled back on the control wheel. The end of the runway flashed underneath, the Archer zoomed skyward in a steep climb.

The sun came back up.

"I think that's so neat!" she whooped.

The Archer's speed dropped. At 75 mph, Margaret pushed the nose down to a level attitude, reduced the power to a cruising rpm and retracted the flaps. Then she cranked the airplane into a steep turn to the left.

"If we hurry," she said with a smile, "we can make the sun rise one or two more times."

"Go for it," I replied, releasing my mint.

Margaret did a quick pre-landing check on the downwind leg and called the controller. "Victor Golf Hotel is downwind Runway 24, requesting a double touch and go."

There was no other traffic in the circuit.

"Victor Golf Hotel is cleared for a touch and go and a touch and go Runway 24, wind 250 at five."

"Victor Golf Hotel, roger."

Margaret kept her circuit in tight. She dove the Archer for the ground on the base leg with the power still on. This was her standard approach, when we flew together. She turned to line up with the runway in the dive. This made the sun set. She wrinkled her nose in delight. Then she cut the power to idle and glided all the way to the runway, trading airspeed for lift, extending the flaps on the way.

We touched down on the numbers. I clinched my mint and braced. Margaret added full power, lifted the Archer into the air, accelerated level to the halfway point of the mile-long runway and then pulled the nose skyward. The airplane clawed for altitude. The sun rose again, this time not quite as high.

"Overshoot! That should get the sun up once more."

We floated in near zero gravity as my pilot pushed the nose over into a descent and cut the power back. The Archer tucked its nose down and headed for the runway. The sun set again.

I could see that there wasn't enough runway remaining for another touch and go. So could Margaret.

"Overshoot?" I asked. "That should get the sun up once more."

"OK."

She reapplied full power and raised the nose to level. The Archer accelerated.

"I check you are in the overshoot, Victor Golf Hotel," the controller said, "call on the downwind."

Margaret pushed the transmit button on her control wheel. "Victor Golf Hotel, roger."

"Fly the airplane first," I reminded her. "Talking can wait."

She knew. She answered me by wrinkling her nose and pointing the airplane up.

This time we saw half of a sunrise in the darkening pink sky before Margaret had to push over at low speed. As she did, a deer mouse popped its head and shoulders out of the defroster slot at the base of the windshield on the pilot's side. The little creature had large, pink-lined ears, a twitchy nose, a white chest and pink front feet. Its beady eyes stared straight at Margaret.

"Oh!" she exclaimed with a sharp intake of breath.

"Squeak!" the mouse peeped.

I lunged for the tiny rodent. Margaret had a different idea. She yanked back on the control wheel. The sudden g force pushed the mouse back into the slot. I missed it.

"Oh! Oh!" Margaret squealed. She looked at her feet and smartly snapped her legs together.

"Fly the airplane," I cautioned. "The mouse can't get into the cabin except through the defroster." It was a lie until I shut off the defroster control.

"Oh! Now what?" she cried in a high-pitched voice.

"Push over into a dive," I said.

Margaret pushed timidly on the wheel.

"More!"

She shoved the nose down. I placed my hand by her defroster vent. The g load came off. The mouse popped up from the defroster slot but this time it was on my side. This surprised all three of us. Margaret pulled the controls back to stop the dive. Mousy ducked below the panel.

"Do the porpoising once more," I said to Margaret.

She did.

This time I had both hands ready, one at each vent. The ears, nose and

79

eyes appeared on my side. It was enough. I caught the terrified intruder barehanded with my thumb and forefinger around its neck. I lifted it from the slot and clamped its body in my hand.

The mouse screamed, "Squeak, squeak!"

"Oh! Oh!" Margaret cried. She shrank against her side of the cockpit. Her eyes were riveted on the head wriggling in my right hand.

"Open your window," I said, pointing at the small opening beside her.

Her eyes popped wider. "Why?" she exclaimed.

"I'll give it a flying lesson."

"No!" she declared. "Don't kill it!" To emphasize, she let go of the controls and covered the vent window with her left arm. The Archer headed for the ground.

"Fly the airplane!" I barked.

Margaret grabbed the wheel and stopped the dive.

John in the control tower was watching. "Victor Golf Hotel, are you experiencing difficulty?"

Margaret looked at me for a response.

"Tell him we're OK and will circle for a full stop landing."

She did.

"You are cleared to land Runway 24, Victor Golf Hotel, wind 240 at five to 10."

"Victor Golf Hotel," Margaret replied.

The mouse continued to squirm. It hadn't bitten me or deposited anything into my hand, yet.

"What should I do with Mickey?"

"Oh! I don't want you to kill him." She looked at the big ears and beady eyes struggling in my hand. "Put him in something until we get on the ground."

I looked around the cockpit and found an airline-type sick bag in the pocket behind the pilot's seat. I opened it with one hand and stuffed the furry passenger into it with the other. I quickly folded the top over and bent the wire tabs to hold it closed.

Margaret had been half watching me and half flying the airplane. "Thank you," she said.

"You're welcome."

I reached back and placed the bag on the seat behind me. Margaret tried to look at it and fly at the same time. The Archer started turning right.

I pointed forward. "You fly. I'll make sure it doesn't get out," I assured her.

"But won't he suffocate in there?" she asked.

"Oh, yes," I replied. "I mean... oh no, at least not until we land."

Margaret cranked her circuit in tight and dove for the runway.

It crossed my mind, while I monitored the flying, that bachelor mice didn't nest in airplanes. This would be a family mouse. I kept one eye on the defroster outlets but I didn't share the information.

My rodent-loving pilot touched the Archer's nosewheel on the numbers at speed. The mainwheels were still in the air. This would create trouble for most pilots but not Margaret. It was her version of a long landing. She cut the power and held the nosewheel on the centreline as the speed bled off and the mainwheels came down. She braked as we approached the intersection and then turned off the runway.

I imagined that Margaret would insist that I release the rodent into the wild, like into the long grass behind the office. From there it would find its way back to her airplane or into someone else's.

I was wrong.

We left the Archer on the ramp in front of the hangar. I walked with Margaret as she hobbled to the office and helped her up the steps. I was carrying the bag.

"Give him some air," Margaret said, once we were in the office, "but please don't let him out."

Summer was following this from behind the flight desk. Normally she would have discreetly taken the sick bag from me for disposal. She gave me a questioning look.

I held up the bag. "We caught a mouse in the airplane," I said.

Her eyes lit up and she leaned forward. "May I see it?" she asked.

I placed the bag on the counter. Summer carefully squeezed the middle of it closed with both hands. I slowly undid the top. Margaret stepped back.

Summer peaked inside and made a small opening with her hands. "Ahhh..., he's so cute." She looked at Margaret. "What are you going to do with him?"

"Oh, I don't know. I'm a little afraid of mice."

"Do you want me to keep him for you?"

"Would you?" Now it was Margaret's eyes that were lighting up.

"Sure. He'll be company in the dorm when I'm studying."

I rolled my eyes. Both women ignored me.

"What will you keep him in?" Margaret asked.

"The pet store will have a cage for him."

"You could pick up a bag of mice chow while you're there," I suggested sarcastically.

"Would they have that?" Margaret asked.

Chapter Fifteen

The gigolo

I was listening to another aviation college graduate. Sergio Santini had breezed into The Flying Circus, introduced himself to me and declared, "I'm just what you're looking for in a flying instructor."

Santini was dressed in a white silk shirt and black dress pants. They were strategically wrinkled to look expensively casual. His dark hair was slicked back like a movie star's. A flashy gold necklace decorated his puffed-out chest and a diamond stud was making a statement in his left earlobe.

"Sergio, what makes you think we need a flying instructor?" I asked.

"Call me Serge," he said. "Every flying school needs an instructor like me."

"How is that?"

"I'll bring in my own students, sell them pilot supplies, charter flights and airplanes. I'll have all their friends and family learning how to fly. You'll be really busy when I get rolling. You can't afford not to have me working here."

"What level is your instructor rating?"

"I haven't actually taken the instructor's course yet," he replied casually.

"Serge, we don't need a flying instructor who is not qualified."

"So you're interested," he responded confidently.

"I didn't say that!"

"You said I just need the instructor rating."

The youngster was too slick for me. Before I lost my cool, I tried to think how Henry would handle him.

"Serge, we are well set up to teach the instructor's course," I offered. "You are welcome to take it here."

"I don't really have time for it," Serge replied.

"With hard work, you can do the course in six weeks," I said.

He smiled. "Does that mean I'm hired?"

"Every flying school needs an instructor like me."

"What do you think?" I asked. The question didn't slow him down.

"Well, I just finished aviation college. I've got student loans, I need income and I know how to generate it, here."

"Without an instructor rating?"

"Yes! Hire me now. I can take that to the bank to pay for the instructor course."

"Hire you to do what?"

"Sell. I'll sell sightseeing flights, flying lessons, charter flights, airplanes and whatever else you do here."

"Banner towing and aerial photography."

"Yes! I'll sell those too. I have a Commercial Pilot Licence. I can fly sightseers, banners and photographers."

"How much experience do you have on tailwheel aircraft?"

"Tailwheel, nosewheel; they're airplanes" he replied. "I fly them all."

"Our main business is instructing."

"You hire me. I take a letter to the bank, get money, pay for the course and teach flying."

"What if your employment here doesn't work out?"

Serge rocked back on his heels and grabbed his chest. "You're breaking my heart!" he exclaimed. "It'll never happen. If it does, fire me and I'll go somewhere else."

That gave me an idea. "Would you take an aptitude test?"

He frowned. "For what?"

"For instructing."

"Oh, sure." He flipped a pen out of his pocket and said, "I'll take it now."

Leanne had been listening to our conversation. She pulled out a copy of Henry's test and placed it on the counter. Serge helped himself to a coffee and sat down at a briefing table. I gave him the test. It took him five minutes.

"This was easy," he declared. "I got 100 per cent."

I looked at the sheet. He had circled 'a' for every answer.

"Serge, you failed. The correct answers for potential flying instructors are all 'c'."

"What!" His voice shot up an octave. "Let me see that."

He grabbed the test from me and read the first line. "When did you decide to become a flying instructor?" He looked up. "When I discovered there are no other flying jobs for new pilots."

"When was that?" I asked.

"Last week."

He looked at the sheet again. "How many model airplanes did you build? Do you want a boy with toys or a man into selling, flying and money?"

I suspected there were a few other things that he left out like sex and drugs. I didn't say anything.

"How many model airplanes did you help others build? Give me a break! I played with the girls. Still do. I'm a natural-born instructor."

I was right.

"Which would be your favourite movie? There is no better flying flick than Top Gun.

"If you were allowed to visit an airline cockpit in flight. Ha! I'd be showing the pilots how to fly the plane. Who wouldn't?

"The first thing you do with something new is. Try it out, of course. Like when you meet a girl.

"How many organizations have you volunteered for? Do you want a Boy Scout or a pilot? I fly and leave the chanting to the sissies.

"How recently have you looked at a textbook? Textbooks are for school. I read mine at the beginning of each semester and then sold them for a profit.

"How many speeding tickets?" Serge grinned. "When the cops ask for my licence, I show them my pilot licence.

"What minimum salary would you accept? I'm not greedy but I need at least $40,000 a year. I plan to make more."

Just what we need, I said to myself, an over-sexed, smart-assed, show-off, party animal.

He handed the sheet back to me and looked at his watch. "I've got a few things to do but I can start today."

"Serge, I appreciate your enthusiasm," I said, "but I can't see things working out for you here."

"I'll tell you what," Serge said. "Hire me. Pay me straight commission; fifteen per cent of the revenue I generate plus the regular pilot salary per hour for flying sightseeing, banner towing and aerial photography."

"We already have a commercial pilot graduate from your college on the instructor course," I said. "He gets first crack at the sightseeing flights. He is also the next to be hired when we need another instructor."

Serge frowned. "What's his name?"

"Icabod Brinsmead."

"What! You hired Pinocchio?"

Chapter Sixteen

The deal

I told Sergio Santini that we'd think about his offer. I asked for his phone number.

"I don't have one," he said. "I'm staying at a girlfriend's and I don't know how long she'll last. I'll call you."

Leanne and I filled Henry in about Serge, his proposal and his test results.

"The guy is cocky," I said.

"Cocky isn't half of it!" Leanne exclaimed. "I wouldn't leave him alone with my daughter for a second!"

"So why are we talking about him?" Henry asked.

Leanne and I looked at each other for the answer.

"I guess because he's a go-getter," I suggested. "He's willing to work on straight sales commissions and flying time while taking the instructor course."

Henry waited. I wasn't convincing him.

"It's an offer that's hard to refuse," I added.

"It sounds like I could refuse him," Henry said. "Icabod is coming along on the instructor's course. I think he'd fit in here better than Sergio the gigolo."

I had to agree, as strange as Icabod was. "OK, I'll let Mr. Santini know that we're not interested. I'll have to wait until he calls."

Serge was too smart to phone. The next day a parade of young people began visiting The Flying Circus office. They inquired about sightseeing flights and flying lessons. "Would Serge Santini be my pilot?" they asked.

"He doesn't work here," Leanne told them.

They declined to schedule flights.

Two days later, Serge came into the office. Henry and I were flying. Leanne related the conversation to us afterward.

"You're looking good today," Serge said to Leanne.

"Thank you," she replied. "Our chief pilot wants to talk to you. He'll be back in an hour."

"OK," he replied, leaning casually on the counter. "How's business?"

"Not bad," she replied.

"Are you getting lots of inquiries about sightseeing flights and lessons?"

"Yes, we are," the receptionist said. "Your friends ask lots of questions but they don't book any flights. It's been good practice answering them but I think I'm up to speed enough that you can call them off."

Serge frowned. "Oh?" was all he said. Then he played his next card. "I know some businesses interested in aerial advertising. May I take a rate card?"

"Certainly," Leanne said. "Then you can answer their questions instead of me. Here, take several."

"Thank you. I can't stay but I'll be in touch."

Serge returned the next day. He flashed a cheesy grin and waved an aerial advertising brochure at Leanne. "I got something for you," he said.

"Oh?"

"This is a signed contract for banner advertising. I'm ready to fly!"

"I'll get Henry from the hangar," Leanne replied.

She went outside and found her husband working on an airplane. "Sergio Santini is here, Henry. He wants to fly some aerial advertising that he sold."

"What did you tell him?"

"That you'd talk to him."

Leanne told me later that Serge dropped his grin as soon as he saw Henry with a no-nonsense look on his face.

"Good afternoon, sir," the youngster said, extending his hand. "It's a pleasure to meet you."

"Likewise, Sergio," Henry replied. "I understand from Leanne that you haven't talked to our chief pilot since giving him your proposal."

"That's why I'm here, sir." He waved the brochure without handing it over. "I'd like to become part of your fine organization starting with this large banner towing contract."

"Well, we appreciate your interest," Henry replied, "but we are not in a position to take advantage of it right now."

Henry's wording left Serge scratching his head.

"Ahh... I..., there's over a thousand dollars worth of banner towing here," he sputtered. He held up the brochure again.

Henry smiled. "I appreciate that Sergio, but we're not in a position to take advantage of it. Not yet."

"Why not?" Serge asked, his smooth voice wavering. "I sold it and I'll fly it. You just count the money and pay me some of it."

"Do you have a couple of minutes?" Henry asked.

"Ahh... yah, sure."

"Good. Have a seat over here," he said.

He sat the young entrepreneur down at a briefing table in the corner. "Are you interested in running this place?" Henry asked.

The question caught Serge off guard. He squirmed. He wanted to say, 'Yes,' but he suspected that it was the wrong answer.

It was.

"I can sell, I can fly and I could run this place if you want me too."

Henry shook his head back and forth. "There are already three people managing it now, Sergio, we don't need you for that."

"Well, I have some ideas..."

Henry held up his hand for silence. Serge stopped talking.

"We don't need you to fly banners either. We have three experienced Super Cub pilots."

Serge opened his mouth. Henry's hand went up before he could speak. He closed it.

"We don't need you to fly sightseers. We have Icabod for that."

Serge bit his tongue and frowned.

"Our training business is picking up. We need more flying instructors. Then the rest of us can tow the banners and run this operation."

Serge held up his hand to speak. Henry waved him off.

"If you'd like to teach flying and get paid, listen up. I'm going to make you an offer. When I'm done, you can take it or leave it, no 'ifs', 'ands' or 'buts'."

"May I say something?"

"No."

Silence.

"I want you to sell for us, everything that we sell: sightseeing flights, flying lessons, charter flights, banner towing, aerial photography, hangar storage, tie-down rent, airplane washing and pilot supplies. You'll receive a five per cent commission paid as a non-refundable credit on your account toward your Instructor Course."

"But, but..."

"No 'buts'. Your account will not be credited until the products and services have been supplied and paid for."

"I... I..."

Henry moved his hand. Serge stopped sputtering.

"You are being hired for sales only," Henry continued. "The credit on your account will be valid only on the Instructor Course. You have six weeks to finish it. If you don't, the remaining credit will be erased."

Serge shook his head back and forth but did not say anything.

"If you pass within the time limit, we'll talk about your teaching here on salary. This deal may be terminated without cause or notice by you, Leanne, my partner or myself. Do you have any questions?"

Leanne told me that the last time she'd heard Henry sound that tough was when their puppy peed in his toolbox. "I was starting to feel sorry for Serge," she said.

The youngster was no puppy. He held up the aerial advertising brochure. "At five per cent, I only get 50 bucks on this contract, and not until the end of the month, if I'm lucky. I need ten per cent."

"No," Henry replied. "Anything else?"

Serge started thinking ahead. "May I continue to sell when I'm instructing?"

"Sergio, focus! Get qualified first!"

"How about a cash advance on my commissions?"

"No!"

"How am I supposed to eat?"

"You're smart. You'll figure it out. Do we have a deal?"

"There are some details we should discuss."

"Leanne is in charge of details. And there will be no disputes."

"I don't like it."

"Good!" Henry said. He stood up. "I was hoping you wouldn't. I think you'd be a pain in the ass working here. You have an Olympic attitude in a small business that rewards hard work. You won't get far. You either walk away now, or take the offer and prove me wrong." He turned to leave.

"I... I think I'll take it." Serge said.

"Now or never?"

Serge hung his head for a second and then stood up. He stuck out his right hand. "Deal."

Henry reached over the table and shook it. "Deal."

Serge forced a smile. "Thank you... I think."

"Work hard and you won't regret it," Henry replied. "Leanne will give you our sales information."

"I have it already."

"Good. Get yourself a pager. We need to contact you anytime, day and night."

"May I trade the pager company for banner advertising?"

The question made Henry smile. "Now you're cooking. You can have one contra ad per company supplying your working needs provided you assemble and set up each one. We'll show you how. Anything else?"

"No. It's time to boogey."

Chapter Seventeen

Call God

I returned from a lesson with a student. Henry was flying. Leanne was fussing behind the flight desk, busting to tell me something. I made another booking with my customer and outlined his next lesson.

"Did Henry talk to you about hiring Sergio Santini?" she asked, as soon as my student had cleared the door.

"Ahh... yes...?" The question surprised me. Leanne had the ironclad memory of a mother. "You were here, remember? We decided not to."

"That was days ago," she frowned. "I mean this morning."

"No. We didn't talk about it this morning."

"Well, Serge came in while you were flying. Henry spoke to him." She watched for my reaction. "He hired him as a salesman."

A mental picture of slippery Serge trying to impress my practical partner made me smile. "I'm sorry I missed it," I said.

"I thought you'd be surprised that he didn't discuss it first," Leanne said. "I was."

"If Henry took him on, he'll know how to make it work," I chuckled. "It would have been fun watching Serge trying to weasel Henry."

"I can't believe how you two run a business without talking to each other!" Leanne declared. Her voice carried the tone of a frustrated wife.

"We don't need to talk," I replied. "Great minds think alike."

Her deepening frown told me that it wasn't the right response.

"Well, your silent partner's great idea for keeping Serge on a leash was to have him report to me!"

Serge Santini was broke and in debt. He did not have his own place, his own phone or transportation. He lived in the residence at Circus University in the room vacated by his former girlfriend. He mooched meals, clothes and rides wherever he could.

Within 24 hours of making the deal with Henry, Serge was fed, mobile and in touch. He traded one-time aerial advertising flights with a pager provider, a restaurant and a taxicab company.

This created our first problem with the slick new salesman. Assembling an advertising banner for a new customer was work. It required organization, attention to detail and actual labour. The seven-foot by three-foot, red, fabric letters were stored on pegs along an inside wall of the hangar. The sides of each letter were clipped to seven-foot fibreglass poles with 14 fasteners. The letters were attached to each other to create a message. A maximum-sized advertisement was 28 characters.

To fly a banner, the assembly was rolled up and driven out to the airport infield. There, all 80 feet of it was laid out, front to back, on the grass. The beginning was hooked to a 200-foot rope which was attached to a loop strung across two, vertical, ten-foot poles. The pilot flew a low pass over the poles trailing a small grappling hook on the end of a 50-foot cable. If he did everything right, the hook plucked the loop off the poles. As he climbed with full power, the rope and then the message peeled of the grass from beginning to end.

Henry had required Serge to assemble each banner when he traded advertising for products and services that he needed. "He'll appreciate the work that goes into them," Henry explained. "Then he won't give away too many ads."

My partner showed the young entrepreneur how to clip the letters and poles together and left him to it. Serge came into the office twenty minutes later.

"Hey, boss, can you check my work?"

My partner and I went out to the hangar. The banner looked like it had been put together by a drunken monkey. Some letters were up side down, some were backward. The clips on most were half done and misaligned like a shirt buttoned by the same monkey.

It took the three of us an hour to undo and redo the message.

"Gee boss," Serge whined, "I just can't get the hang of this."

The kid probably messed up on purpose. Henry stood his ground. "We don't have time for this, Serge. You'll have to do it right or that's the end of your contra deals."

Serge and Icabod Brimsmeade had been classmates in college. Socially they were at the opposite ends of the scale. Serge had partied his way through school.

"I passed, barely," he happily admitted one day. "It took a lot of smooth talking." Then he laughed. "I was helped by inside information on the questionable activities of two instructors."

Apparently, Icabod's marks and flying were not that great either. He was born a gardener but wanted to be a pilot. He graduated from the course by memorizing everything and flying by the book.

The banner looked like it had been put together by a drunken monkey.

Icabod couldn't sell a peanut to a starving elephant but he knew the value of hard work. His immigrant parents ran a small greenhouse operation near the airport. Their son grew up in the family business, working before and after school.

Serge and Icabod had three things in common. Both were penniless, had no transportation and they both wanted to fly. Otherwise they were so different that I couldn't imagine them working together.

Icabod lived at home. He worked in the greenhouses for eight hours starting at six a.m. Then he walked to The Flying Circus for instructor lessons with Henry each afternoon.

I was in the office when the former classmates met at The Flying Circus for the first time.

Icabod had just come in from a flight with Henry. Serge breezed through the door.

"Hey, Icky, how's it going, pal?"

Icabod's face turned red. Serge grabbed his hand and shook it vigorously.

"Fine, Sergio," he replied meekly.

"Say, Ick, I'm working in the hangar. Have you got a minute?"

"Soo... soon. I have to finish with Mr. Rains."

"Sure, sure. Take your time. I'll grab a coffee while I'm waiting."

An hour later, Serge had Icabod finishing the banner that he had been working on and had all of us convinced that it was a good idea.

"The kid's a whiz," Serge proclaimed. He was drinking another coffee while Icabod made banners in the hangar. "He can count, spell and he's a natural with those stupid little clips. I'll apply some of my commission to his account for making and setting up every ad I sell."

We agreed.

Icabod had six jobs by the end of the week. From Monday to Friday he started in the greenhouses. At the airport he did his instructor course and assembled banners. On Saturday he set up banners for us to fly and washed airplanes, a service that Serge sold to local aircraft owners. In between, Icabod flew sightseers over Niagara Falls in response to coupons that Serge's friends had spread throughout the city.

"The kid's doing OK," Serge commented to me from the couch on Saturday. "Tomorrow I've got two banners for him and three airplane washes."

"Serge, Icabod goes to church on Sundays."

"Yah, in the morning. I've got him lined up all afternoon."

"No, Serge, he and his family attend church all day on Sundays."

"What do you mean, 'all day'? Nobody goes to church all day!"

"The Brimsmeades do, sunup to sundown. Icabod won't be here tomorrow."

"But he's got to work tomorrow! We need him here! Who do I call?"

"You could try God but you probably don't have his number."

Chapter Eighteen

Spun

I had met a girl named Carol. We were similar ages and both single. She was attractive and I was interested. She wasn't my girlfriend, yet. We hadn't actually been on a date.

Carol was a country girl. She taught public school outside of the nearby town of Derry. She had the smarts and depth of character to be comfortable with herself. She was not the type to respond to blunt males. I couldn't phone her and say, "Hey, how about I grab a pizza and come over to your place for some one-on-one?"

I needed a reason to call.

Leanne mentioned that Henry was taking her and the kids to a fireworks display. "At the waterfront park tomorrow night," she said.

"Sounds like fun."

"It will be the closest thing to a date in a long time," she sighed. "He's trying to make up for hiring Serge and passing him off on me."

I was half listening. "Ahh, huh," I replied.

I was thinking of Carol. I checked the scheduling sheets. Tomorrow was my day to work late but there were just two bookings, both in Cherokees: one rental and one lesson. The student was working on a Night Endorsement and had already flown solo at night. If the weather was good, I could send him on a solo practice flight. If it was bad, there would be no fireworks. I got on the telephone, first to the customers and then to Carol.

"Hi, Carol? It's me."

"Hello there." Her tone was friendly. "To what do I owe the pleasure of this call?"

That was Carol, country pleasant and schoolteacher direct.

"I was wondering what you are doing tomorrow evening."

"What's up?"

"Well... ahh... there is a fireworks display here in Circus. Would you like to see them with me?" I sounded like a thirteen-year-old calling for

94

his first date.

There was a pause.

"What time?"

"Ahh... just after sunset. I could pick you up around seven thirty?"

"Oh, there is no need for you to drive all this way and back twice. I could meet you there."

Meeting at the fireworks would not be much of a date. I had something more impressive in mind.

"I was... I mean, I thought I'd fly to Derry and pick you up at the airport. We could see the fireworks from the air." We had been on a short flight once before.

"That sounds exciting," she replied. "I'd like that."

"Good. I'll meet you at the Derry Air Flying School at seven thirty. If the weather is bad, maybe we could do something else?"

"Well, we'll see."

"Can I call you tomorrow with an update, say around six o'clock?"

"Fine, I'll talk to you then."

I was happy that she was interested. Then I mentally kicked myself for arranging that I wouldn't be driving her home.

The next evening the weather was good. I called Carol and let her know that the flight was on.

"Great," she replied. "I'll see you at Derry Air around seven thirty."

I left the keys and logbooks in the two Cherokees and pulled out the Cessna 172. Its high wing design was best for sightseeing and Carol could sit next to me.

Barry McDay was working in the Circus Control Tower. "What's in Derry tonight?" he asked, after giving me a taxi clearance.

"A date," I said. Then I winced. Information like that usually became fodder for controllers who had too little to do in the evenings.

"Ooh la la," he replied.

I taxied out and took off.

"Talk to you later, Romeo," Barry said when I was clearing his control zone.

Carol was waiting on the edge of the Derry Air ramp when I taxied in. She was a short, well-featured girl. She looked like a schoolteacher, a soft one, the kind that everyone liked. She was wearing loose slacks and a pretty blouse, done up to the neck. A sweater was draped over her shoulders. Her rounded face glowed in the light of the setting sun.

I climbed out of the pilot side of the Cessna and walked toward her. "Hi! You look very nice this evening."

"Thank you." She blushed a little. "I hope the dress code is casual for

"Talk to you later, Romeo," Barry said as I climbed clear of his zone.

this flight, captain."

"You're fine. It's just you, me and the fireworks."

She didn't offer a hug so I didn't take one. I led her around to the passenger side of the Cessna. She allowed me to help her climb in and fasten her seat belt.

"This is a different airplane," she commented.

"Yes, my LearJet is in the shop," I joked.

She smiled but didn't have a comeback.

I explained a few things as I restarted the engine and called the ground controller. We were given Runway 24. I taxied slowly and completed the pre-take-off checks methodically, the way I hoped would impress my passenger.

"Ready?" I asked beside the runway.

Carol smiled and nodded. "Yes."

The wind was light and there was no other traffic. We were cleared for takeoff. The evening sky was all ours. I turned onto the runway and smoothly applied full power. The sun was sinking below the horizon on our right. The Cessna accelerated politely and lifted gently into the air. The nose came up. I looked at Carol. Her head was bobbing forward and her eyes were closed. Slowly her body slid over until it was slumped against my arm. Her head dropped sideways onto my shoulder. She was sleeping.

The Cessna continued climbing. I had planned to show Carol the sights around Derry on the way to the fireworks but decided to let her snooze. It felt good to have her resting against me. The light scent of her hair mingled with the smell of aging plastic, baking engine oil and fuel vapours. I smiled at this new closeness. It didn't matter that I was the only one who knew about it. I turned the airplane toward Circus.

I placed my hand lightly on Carol's left leg as we approached the Circus Control Zone. She didn't stir. I rubbed gently. She moaned.

"Carol, we're here," I said.

"Ohhhh," she murmured. One eye opened slowly followed by the other. "What... what... where am I?"

I squeezed her leg. She sat up. "It's OK, its OK," I soothed. "You fell asleep as we were flying along."

She blinked several times and looked around. Surprise turned to embarrassment. "Did I really doze off?"

I patted her leg lightly. "Yes, you did. We're approaching Circus now."

She placed her left hand over mine. "I feel foolish."

"Don't be. You behaved yourself."

I could see her face redden in the pale cockpit light. She covered it with her other hand. "I'm sorry," she said.

"It's OK."

The first of the fireworks appeared ahead. I squeezed her leg again. "I didn't want you to miss the action," I said. "Have a look."

She took her hand off her face. A double starburst erupted about five miles in front of us.

"Wow!" she exclaimed, perking up.

I nodded in agreement and picked up the microphone.

"Circus Tower, this is Cessna Lima Uniform Foxtrot Tango, approaching your zone from Derry at 2,000 feet, request clearance to circle over the waterfront."

The fireworks continued. Carol leaned forward to get a better look. The Cessna dipped its nose in response to her movement. I added back pressure to the control wheel to maintain our altitude.

"It's beautiful," she said, squeezing my hand.

"Cessna Lima Uniform Foxtrot Tango," Barry replied from the tower, "altimeter 30.08. I have a Cherokee in the circuit on Runway 24 and another Cherokee circling the lakeshore at 1,500 feet. You are cleared into the zone along the shoreline. Suggest you stay at 2,000. Go ahead your next intended destination."

"Uniform Foxtrot Tango will remain at 2,000 along the shoreline, then proceed to Niagara Falls. We'll be landing back at Derry."

"Roger Uniform Foxtrot Tango. Call established over the fireworks."

"Uniform Foxtrot Tango."

At the beach park I rolled the airplane into a shallow bank to the right. I had to pull harder on the controls to hold altitude but I didn't want to give up the cozy hand over hand on Carol's leg to adjust the elevator trim.

I spotted the lights of the Cherokee. It was circling in the opposite direction underneath us. I shifted my right knee and pressed it against the microphone in its holder below the throttle.

"Uniform Foxtrot Tango is established at 2,000, traffic in sight," I called out.

It worked.

"Uniform Foxtrot Tango, roger," Barry replied. "Are you keeping your hands to yourself?" he asked.

I kneed the transmit button again. "Are you?"

If Carol followed the exchange, she didn't let on. She turned and looked out her side window. The lights of the city rotated below. Boaters watching from the harbour displayed a carpet of navigation lights on the water. The fireworks spiraled up and exploded in the middle of this show. It was a scene that I hoped would impress my date.

Carol instinctively leaned back against me. "They look so close."

"Don't worry," I said. "We are much higher than the fireworks can reach."

I could feel Carol's body relax during our second circle. After a par-

Carol didn't stir. My right arm went numb but I didn't mind.

ticularly bright burst of pyrotechnics, I said. "That was a good one."

There was no reply. I bent my head forward to look at Carol's face. Her eyes were closed. I squeezed her leg. There was no response. I rolled the Cessna out of the turn and headed for Derry. I reached over with my left hand and turned the volume down on the radio and then I used it to lift the microphone from its holder.

"Circus Tower, Uniform Foxtrot Tango is departing the lakeshore area at 2,000 heading for Derry."

"So soon?" Barry replied. "What happened to Niagara Falls?"

"Not tonight."

"But it's the honeymoon capital of the world."

"I'll call you clear of the zone."

"Why are you whispering?"

I didn't reply.

"Too busy, eh? I have no reported traffic to the west, Uniform Foxtrot Tango. You are cleared enroute."

"Foxtrot Tango."

Carol didn't stir all the way to Derry. My right arm went numb from her weight against it but I didn't mind. I rubbed her leg to wake her up. There was no response.

I spoke softly into her ear. "Carol, we're home."

Nothing.

I picked up the microphone with my left hand. "Derry Tower, Cessna Lima Uniform Foxtrot Tango is approaching your zone from the east at 2,000 feet inbound for landing."

"Cessna Lima Uniform Foxtrot Tango, Derry Tower, I have you in sight, the wind is calm, altimeter 30.09, cleared for a straight in to Runway 12. Call on final."

"Uniform Foxtrot Tango."

The radio chatter didn't rouse Carol. I reached my left hand over to the throttle and reduced the power. The nose dropped and the airplane started to descend. Carol twisted toward me and buried her face in my shoulder but didn't wake up.

I pulled the control wheel back to slow the airplane. Then I hooked my left knee behind it so I could lower some flap with my left hand. It was awkward. Closer in, I was high on the approach. I throttled back some more, lowered the rest of the flap and grabbed for the microphone.

"Uniform Foxtrot Tango on final."

My knee slipped, the Cessna lurched right and the nose pitched down. I dropped the mic and hauled back on the controls. It was a short but wild roller-coaster ride.

"Uniform Foxtrot Tango is cleared to land Runway 12, wind calm."

I didn't try to acknowledge. Carol reached her right arm across my chest and latched onto my left shoulder. We were still too high. I jammed my knee against the back of the controls again and cut the power off with my left hand. The Cessna dropped. The landing light was off but I could see the runway lights rising up quickly. I grabbed the wheel and pulled. The airplane kangarooed into the flare out, skipped first one tire and then another off the runway before finally plopping down for good.

"Uniform Foxtrot Tango is cleared to the ramp," the controller said.

I didn't reply.

Carol began to stir. She wriggled, moaned and frowned but did not wake up.

I taxied to Derry Air and parked. I reached forward with my left hand and pulled the mixture control out. The engine stopped. Carol's eyes fluttered open. She looked at her right arm hugging me and then to my face.

"Welcome back," I said softly.

She let go of my shoulder. "Where are we?"

"At Derry Air."

She straightened up slowly. "What about the fireworks?"

"All done," I replied.

"Did I miss them?"

"Mostly."

Carol rubbed her eyes with her free hand. "I'm sorry. I knew I'd be tired but I didn't want to say, 'No,' when you called."

"I'm glad you came but I guess I picked the wrong day."

Carol looked around. "You must be a smooth pilot if I slept through the landing and everything."

I knew the country schoolteacher was uncomfortable when not in control but I couldn't resist saying, "Thank you, but you don't know the half of it."

She looked at her hand on mine. "What else were you doing smoothly besides flying?"

I gave the leg one last squeeze. "Restraining you," I said.

Her face turned scarlet. She looked at her buttons and then mine. "I don't believe you."

"I'll never tell." I smiled and lifted my hand. "Come on, I'll drive you home."

"You don't have do that. I'll be fine."

"Carol, you feel asleep watching fireworks. I can't let you drive when you're that tired."

"I'm fine, really," she said stubbornly. "I shouldn't have taken the Gravol but they're wearing off now. I'll have supper when I get home and be as good as new." She forced a smile.

"You were afraid of being airsick so you skipped supper and took

Gravol instead? It's a wonder you woke up at all."

"Oh, it's not the pills or lack of food that made me sleepy. It's a whole year teaching a split Grade 2/3. Today was the last day of school."

"I'll drive you home, drive back here and leave your car. You can catch a cab to pick it up in the morning."

She leaned over and gave me a peck on the cheek. "You're sweet, but I'll be OK. The top is down on the MG. The fresh air will keep me awake." She unbuckled her seat belt and opened her door. "Come on, walk me to my car. If I don't fall, I can drive."

I walked her to the sports car. She didn't fall. I slid my arms around her before she got in. She turned toward me. I bent down. She let me kiss her full on the lips. It was the worst kiss I have ever tasted.

Chapter Nineteen

Double talk

"There's a registered letter here for you from the government," Leanne said. She held out a piece of paper.
I read it.

> Dear Sir;
> It has come to our attention that on June 19th you were the pilot of Piper Super Cub Charlie Sierra Charlie Uniform Bravo registered to The Flying Circus. This aircraft was allegedly engaged in Aerial Medevac activities at Collingwood, Ontario in contravention of the Air Transportation Act.
> You are required to submit the company's original daily flight log covering June 19th and the current Aircraft Journey Logbook within 30 days of the date on this letter to support an investigation into this alleged contravention.
> Sincerely,
> Cam I. Kazie
> Chief of Aviation Enforcement, Ontario Region

"June 19 was the day I flew aerial photos near Collingwood with Snappy."

"Right," Leanne said. "You also flew a sick guy to the Collingwood Airport,"

"Sure, and I ran into Inspector Kennedy. Has Henry seen this?" My partner's mind worked better than mine on bureaucratic business.

"Not yet, he's flying."

I talked to Henry after he read the letter.

"We never received money for that medevac flight," I said, "so we are in the clear, right?"

"You'd think so but technically it was a medevac for which we are not licenced. Payment is not the issue."

"It was a mercy flight."

"If you're Inspector Kennedy, it was a zero-dollar medevac."

"Oh, great! Now what?"

"I don't think it's a big deal. I'll send a letter with the documents. We should be able to nip this in the bud."

"I'm not so sure because Kennedy is involved. I was thinking that the bird hunters were rich guys from Toronto. Snappy took their picture. If we could find out who they are, it might give us some leverage."

"All right. I'll draft a letter. You call Don Hitchcock. Maybe he knows them."

"Good idea."

Don Hitchcock was a local lawyer, a member of the provincial parliament and a cabinet minister. We leased the Super Cub from him. He purchased it so we could tow banners for his re-election campaign. I left a message at his office in Toronto to call me.

"What's up?" Don said. "Hee, hee. Did you get it?"

Don was a joker.

"Hi, Don. Yes I did, thank you. Listen, I have a problem that maybe you can help me with."

"Go ahead, fly it by me, hee, hee."

I described my encounter at Pheasant Island and the subsequent medevac flight. "The sick guy's name was George. He and his buddies had been drinking like lawyers all morning. I wondered if you knew them."

"Hey, what's wrong with drinking in the morning?" Don asked. He was chuckling.

"Nothing if you can handle it. George couldn't."

"Was he short, balding, old and fat like me?"

"Yes."

"That sounds like George Bartholomew. He represents one of the Toronto ridings in the legislature, for the wrong party. He sits on the opposite side of the House. George is a man of small talent and simple needs. If he had a motto, it would be: 'If it moves in the woods, shoot it; if it's fattening, eat it; and if it's work, ignore it.' Was he with a tall, belligerent, sausage-faced guy named Sandy?"

"One of them was tall and belligerent," I replied. "I didn't get his name."

"That's Sanderson Lysander, George's lawyer buddy and a low-life influence peddler."

I told Don about our pending medevac violation. "We'd have to be sure it was the same guy before we got him involved," I said.

"I'll check it at this end."

"Henry, this is great. How do you think up stuff like this?"

The next day, Henry showed me his letter.

> Cam I. Kazie
> Chief of Aviation Enforcement,
> Ontario Region
>
> Dear Sir;
> Thank you for your attention to the matter of a mercy
> flight conducted by The Flying Circus.
> It would appear that the air regulations do not accommo-
> date a situation where a commercial pilot, flying for a com-
> mercial air service, not licenced for medevac activities, may
> assist someone who is suddenly sick or injured to reach med-
> ical attention quickly.
> I look forward to the government's solution to this over-
> sight. If there is anything further that we can do to help,
> please let us know. In the meantime, we will continue con-
> ducting mercy flights as a public service should the need
> arise again.
> Sincerely,
> Henry Rains
> The Flying Circus

"Henry, this is great. How do you think up stuff like this?"
"I worked for the school board, remember? There was a big need for crafting replies in double-talk."
"I'm glad you're on our side."

Don Hitchcock called me back the next morning. He was excited. "You won't believe it!" he whooped. "I put our press secretary on this and he hit the jackpot. It was George Bartholomew and his slime-ball buddy Sandy Lysander at the Pheasant Island Hunt Club on June 19. Now get this: the third guy was the National Director of Airports for Aviation Transportation in Ottawa! I bet they were cooking up construction deals for the Toronto Airport that would benefit Lysander's clients and Bartholomew's riding.

"Wow!"

"Wow is right. When this gets out, you won't have to worry about your violation but George and his buddies will. They'll be in hot water. I can't wait for the government to lay a charge on you. First, we'll call the press and make you the hero of a mercy flight for a certain drunken member of parliament. Then we'll send the cops after Lysander for commandeering the aircraft without paying. Finally, we'll ask the Minister of Transport why his Airports Director was on a freebee hunting junket with known influence peddlers."

"Whoa! Whoa! Hold your horses, Don," I said. "We're just trying to duck a minor missile fired by an overzealous aviation inspector."

"But we'll get you off the hook by going public with a juicy embarrassment for the opposition party."

"Well, can you wait a few days, Don? Henry sent a letter tossing the ball back into their court."

"Boy, just when I was going to have some fun."

"We appreciate everything that you've done, but please hold the national incident. Let's see what the enforcement people do next."

"OK, fly boy, but let me know how you make out as soon as possible. I'll be ready to go to town."

Word must have gotten around the government that Don's press secretary had been digging. Our Daily Flight Log and the Super Cub's Journey Logbook were sent back by courier. There was no explanation attached.

Now I was ticked. "They think they can stir us up with a pending violation," I said to Henry, "and then just drop it like that!"

"Maybe a letter will come separately," he suggested.

None did.

I telephoned the Aviation Enforcement office. A receptionist said that Mr. Kazie was not available to speak to me. I left a message for a return call. Kazie never phoned.

Chapter Twenty

In the flesh

"I need two hours in the Super Cub on Saturday." It was Snappy Shuttlecock on the phone.

"We have banners to tow starting at one o'clock, Snappy. Can we do it before then?"

"We'll have to."

"What are we shooting?"

"Nudes."

"Sounds like fun. Where...?"

He had hung up.

Saturday dawned bright and sunny. I had the Cub ready for I-wasn't-sure-what by 10:30. Snappy arrived across our lawn in his Land Rover. He stopped beside the airplane, jumped out and began yanking camera equipment from of the back of the car.

"Ready to go?" he asked, handing me a heavy leather case. It was full of glass plate negatives.

"Good morning," I replied.

"Good morning."

I leaned into the rear of the Cub and hefted the case into the baggage compartment. "Where are we shooting?" I asked.

"Port Colbourne," he replied. He brushed past me and climbed into the airplane's back seat carrying his aerial camera.

I looked at the Land Rover blocking the ramp.

"Let's go!" Snappy barked.

"I need to sign out and move your car."

"Oh, yah. You sign out," he said, scrambling out of the Cub. He dropped the big camera on the seat. "I'll move the Rover."

I was back in two minutes. Snappy was dancing beside his vehicle madly slapping the multitude of pockets in his camouflage suit. He was searching for his keys. I slid into the Land Rover's driver's seat. I knew the keys were in it because the engine was running. I drove around to the parking lot and jogged back to the ramp. Snappy was sitting in the Cub.

"Thanks," he whistled through his stub of a nose.

He sorted out his camera stuff while I started the Cub, taxied out and took off.

"Tell me what we're doing?" I asked, leveling at 2,000 feet.

"Not much to tell," he replied. "There's a nudist camp on the Lake Erie shore near Port Colbourne. They blocked off the public beach in front of their property and are using it as their own. The police want proof that they are going naked on public property before forcing them to remove the barriers. They don't want to raid the place to find out so you and I are going to take their picture."

I didn't say anything. I was thinking that I should have brought binoculars and a bulletproof vest. I wanted the vest more than the magnifiers. I didn't know Snappy very well. I wondered if his police story was a cover for more commercial purposes.

"It sounds like a sneaky job," I said.

"It pays," the photographer replied.

Snappy leaned forward and showed me the nudist camp location on my map. I headed that way. Twenty minutes later I spotted two large piles of brush blocking the beach. A few pink people were enjoying the sunshine. The rest of the property looked like a regular trailer park in the woods. I pointed it out to Snappy.

"That's it," he said. "Drop down and give me a slow pass along the shoreline east to west. Make it count. They might all run for the trees."

I turned, descended and slowed the Cub.

"Ready for the door?" I called out.

"Ready!"

I opened it and leveled off at 200 feet above the lakeshore.

"Lower!" Snappy yelled over the wind noise in his microphone.

Out of the corner of my eye I could see the camouflaged photographer leaning into the slipstream ahead of the wing struts. Both hands gripped the camera handles. His face was looking down into the viewfinder. I changed hands on the control stick, reached over and grabbed the back of his pants. I eased the Cub down to 150 feet.

"In closer!" Snappy shouted.

I sideslipped toward the shore. There were lots of people on the beach. Some were playing volleyball, others were sunning and a few were digging in the sand with kids. Most looked up at the airplane. Several waved. They were all naked.

We covered their short section of sand quickly.

"That's great!" Snappy declared.

I pulled the Cub into a climbing right turn.

109

"Give me another pass like that but higher. I'll get the whole compound in one frame."

"Each fly-by increases the chance of someone taking a shot at us," I said.

"I didn't see any dangerous weapons, did you?" Snappy laughed into his headset.

I swung the Cub around and flew over the water at 250 feet. More nudists were emerging from the tree line. They shaded their eyes with their hands and waved at us. I didn't wave back.

"Perfect!" Snappy declared. "Let's go home."

The handicapped photographer stumbled into our office with the picture proofs on Monday. "You're going to love these," he declared.

Serge and I joined him at a table. Leanne walked over and closed the door. Henry and Icabod continued practising an instructor's briefing at the blackboard.

Snappy spread an array of photos on the table. They clearly showed young and old people enjoying the beach in their birthday suits. Serge and I each picked one up to look closer. The body details were there.

"Can I get copies of these?" Serge asked.

"Is Inspector Kennedy in any of them?" Leanne inquired, looking over my shoulder.

Snappy tapped my arm with a crooked finger. "Now look through this," he said, handing me a magnifying glass."

It took me a moment to find the right focal depth before an older lady, sunning on her back, filled the glass. I could see everything. She was wearing a skin-coloured bathing suit decorated with body parts.

They all were.

Chapter Twenty-one

"Yes sir"

A rock concert was coming to the football stadium south of Buffalo. Serge landed a banner towing contract for it.

"I don't know if we can do it, Serge," I said.

"Sure, we can," he answered confidently. "I checked." He stepped over to the wall map. "It's 40 miles." He pointed to the stadium location. "That's 35 minutes each way and an hour over the crowd. Time to spare."

Our maximum airtime for towing a banner was three hours. The limit was dictated by fuel and the pilot's bladder capacity.

"I charged the guy for two hours," Serge added. "He was happy. He pre-paid."

"I wasn't thinking of distance," I replied. "Our Aerial Advertising Licence is Canadian, not international."

"No problem. We tow banners in and out of American airspace around Niagara Falls all the time."

He was right.

"Well, I'd better check on it."

"Oh, man!" he moaned. "Don't call the government. They're spring loaded to say 'No' to everything."

"If we don't ask and they don't like it, we could get shut out of Niagara Falls."

"American helicopter companies cross the border on sightseeing flights around The Falls every day. Flying over there has not been a problem. Don't make it one."

Serge was probably right, again. I called anyway.

I talked to the Federal Aviation Administration District Office. I told an inspector that we wanted to tow a banner from Circus to the upcoming rock concert in Buffalo.

"Is that OK with you guys," I asked, "as long as we don't land on the American side?"

"To conduct aerial advertising in the United States, you must have the appropriate American Operating Certificate," was the reply.

"So American helicopter operators in Niagara Falls are licensed by both Canada and the United States to fly sightseers back and forth across the border?"

There was a pause. "I'll have someone get back to you," he said.

I told Serge. "We shouldn't do it without an American Operating Certificate."

"But don't you see? They license the Americans and our government licenses us. They cross over here and we cross over there."

"So if the Cub had extra-long-range tanks, we could tow banners over New York City from here?"

"Absolutely! That's a great idea! You see about the extra fuel and I'll line up the advertisers."

"I don't think so."

"Trust me. Towing into the U.S. from here is not an issue."

I called the Canadian Department of Transport Regional Office and asked the same question. A receptionist took the information and said someone would return my call.

I told Serge.

"The concert is this Saturday," he groaned. "We'll never hear from that bunch in time."

Henry, Leanne and I had a powwow on Friday afternoon. We had not received a call back from either government.

"If we tow the banner into the U.S. and the Americans object," Henry said, "what's the most they can they do? Tell us not to do it again?"

"Possibly," I replied, "but we don't want to jeopardize our right to cross the border on charter flights and with banners at Niagara Falls."

Leanne was more positive. "If they don't object, we could get more stadium advertising for the football season this fall. As your bookkeeper, I'd say that it would be a good thing."

"Inspector Kennedy is already gunning for us," I added. "This might give him more ammunition."

"We are licensed to tow ads in Canada," Henry replied. "I see this as being between us and the Americans."

"Who is this banner for?" I asked.

"A Cadillac dealership," Leanne replied, "in Buffalo."

I winced. "It would be better if it was a Canadian advertiser. Then we wouldn't be competing directly with American companies."

"Perhaps," Henry said, "but I don't see that as the issue. I vote we give it a shot and see what happens."

Leanne nodded in agreement.

"Saturday is your evening to work," Henry said to me. "If you'd rather not do it, I understand. I can fly it for you."

"No. The Super Cub and I are available," I replied. "We are in this together. I'll fly the banner."

"OK," Henry said. "You're booked for lessons before the tow. I'll ask Icabod to stay and set it up for you."

"Thanks. Will you visit me in jail if this blows up into an international incident?"

"Sure, partner," Henry smiled. "If they allow the one phone call, you know my number."

Icabod made up the banner and laid it out on the infield grass Saturday afternoon. I finished with my last student and drove out with him to check it. The banner was perfect and so was the set-up.

"You do good work, Icabod," I said to the timid youngster. "We're lucky to have you."

"Thank you, sir," he replied, looking at his feet. He was wearing running shoes for the first time.

He had also filled the Super Cub with gas and attached the grappling hook cable to the release mechanism under the tail. I looked the Cub over and climbed in. It was six o'clock. I chuckled to myself. Aerial advertising was supposed to be a daylight only operation. Even if the politics of this flight were illegal, I should be back before official dark at nine o'clock.

Icabod made sure that I had no trouble starting the Cub and then drove my car back to the infield.

There was comfort in the fact that the air was cool and there was a light breeze coming from the southwest. The banner pick-up would be easy even with the weight of full fuel and a maximum-sized message. It remained to be seen if anyone would object to a Canadian company flying a commercial banner into the United States.

I taxied out, did my pre-take-off checks and departed on Runway 24. The Cub's door was open. The metal grappling hook and steel cable were in my lap. The rest trailed out the door to the release mechanism.

There was no other traffic. I turned left during the climbout and started a tight circuit. On the downwind, I tossed the hook and cable out, visually checked that it was trailing behind and below the tail and then closed the door.

"Charlie Uniform Bravo is cleared for a low and over parallel to Runway 24," the air traffic controller said. "The wind is 240 at five, occasionally higher."

"Charlie Uniform Bravo."

I could see "GO IN STYLE BUFFALO CADILLAC" laid out in large red letters on the grass. My car was parked nearby. Icabod was standing next to it ready to reset the pick-up poles if I knocked them down.

The flaps remained extended from the takeoff. I throttled back and began a curving descent to line up for a run at the loop strung between the poles. The speed was 85 mph. I leveled off at 30 feet above the ground and held the Cub steady so the hook wouldn't swing wildly.

The airplane cleared the rope. I hauled back on the control stick with my right hand and applied full power with my left. I reached my left hand down onto the release lever on the floor to be ready to dump the load if necessary.

I felt the tug of the hook snagging the rope and lifting the letters off the grass. The Cub slowed. I pushed the stick forward. The speed settled at 75 mph.

"It looks like a clean pick-up, Charlie Uniform Bravo," the controller said. "Call clearing the zone to the south."

"Charlie Uniform Bravo."

I banked the airplane to the left, slid the window open and looked back. The banner was trailing nicely behind. There were no twists or whip snapping. I could see Icabod giving me a 'thumbs up' from below. It was a 'go'. I waved to him. The time was twenty after six.

I pointed the Cub south and climbed slowly to 1,000 feet above the ground. Niagara Falls was on my way to Buffalo so I set course to fly by it for extra exposure.

I timed a speed check over the ground. Serge's estimate of 35 minutes each way was based on no wind. The southwest breeze knocked my ground speed back to 60 mph. It was no big deal. It would add five minutes or so to the trip to the stadium.

Niagara Falls was crawling with tourists. I looked down at sidewalks clogged with slow-moving, ant-sized pedestrians. Tiny cars filled the streets.

I continued to fly southbound along the Niagara River occasionally turning to check on the banner; so far, so good.

The stadium was south of the city and outside the Buffalo Airport Control Zone. I listened to the recorded airport information. The active runway was 23. I was flying below the Terminal Control area but I called anyway. If I wasn't supposed to be there, I wanted someone to tell me. The radio traffic was light.

"Buffalo Terminal, this is a Canadian Piper Super Cub, Sierra Charlie Uniform Bravo with Information Uniform."

"Super Cub Charlie Uniform Bravo, Buffalo Approach, squawk 5312 and say your altitude."

I selected the four-digit code on my transponder. "Charlie Uniform Bravo is level at 1,900 towing a banner to the stadium."

"Charlie Uniform Bravo, radar contact 12 miles west. At 1,900 you are below my airspace. You are cleared on route."

"Charlie Uniform Bravo."

I was soon in American airspace. The banner continued to behave itself. I spotted the stadium floodlights 15 miles away.

The concert's opening act was scheduled to start at seven o'clock. The roads below were filled with brake lights blinking their way toward the stadium.

I started my first circle of the open air gathering at five minutes after seven. I played it safe by flying outside the perimeter of the seats. We had a banner break loose once so I wanted to be over the surrounding parking lot rather than the stands. It was no penalty for our advertiser. Our extra large letters could be read up to a mile away. I stayed high. At 1,900 feet, I was about 1,100 feet above the ground. No one could fault me for creating a hazard.

I checked the Cub's systems and the banner regularly. There was no other air traffic but I turned on all my lights and monitored the Buffalo Approach frequency anyway.

I saw the opening band come onto the stage. The stands were about one third full but that was changing quickly. Sunset was an hour away but I could make out a constant twinkle of camera flashes. One of the musicians must have been using a metal body grinder. He was sending showers of sparks into the air in different directions. I was glad that I couldn't hear it.

A Cessna 172 appeared towing a banner in the opposite direction. It was flying well below me and inside my circles. The letters were much smaller than ours. I couldn't read the backward message but I had fun trying. I watched for other aircraft to join us but none did. The Cessna disappeared after a while but I didn't see it leave.

I continued around the concert until the sun disappeared below the horizon and then headed home. It was 8:30.

I didn't radio anyone until I called the Circus Tower approaching the control zone.

"Circus, Charlie Uniform Bravo is six miles south at 1,300 inbound for the banner drop."

"Charlie Uniform Bravo, Circus Tower, confirm you are six miles south of Circus towing a banner?"

"Affirmative. I'll flash my landing light."

"I have you in sight, Charlie Uniform Bravo. Continue for a left base for a banner drop south and parallel to Runway 24, wind calm, altimeter 29.98. Confirm you still have the complete banner."

I opened my window, skidded the Cub with left rudder and looked behind. I couldn't make out the individual letters in the failing light but the banner was trailing straight which told me that the aerodynamic tail was still attached.

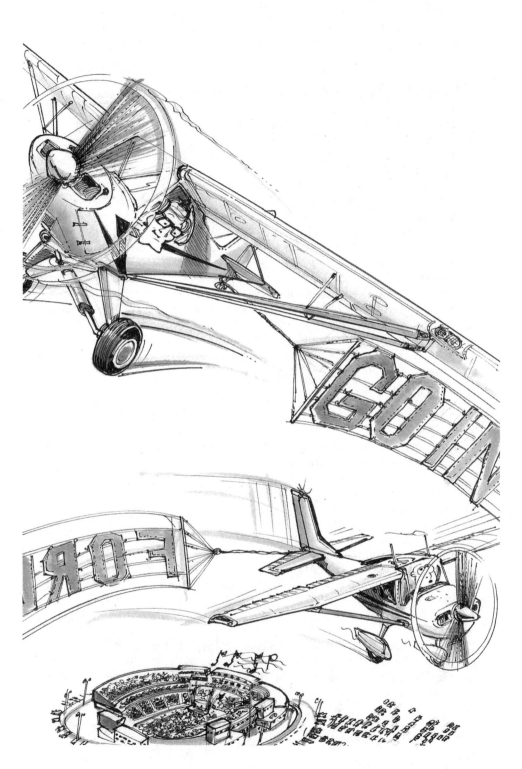

A Cessna 172 appeared towing a banner in the opposite direction.

"Affirmative, Uniform Bravo. I'll call you on the left base for the drop."

The confirmation was a strange request. I knew all of the controllers in the Circus Tower. I also knew that they wouldn't tell me much on the frequency.

I got busy descending and completing my pre-landing check. I could see flashing taillights in the infield. Icabod must have stayed, even though I had told him to go home. He was marking the drop zone in the twilight with my car.

"Charlie Uniform Bravo is cleared for a low and over the infield south of Runway 24, wind calm. Check the vehicle in the grass. Call on the downwind for landing."

"Uniform Bravo."

I descended, turned and lined up between the Volkswagen and the runway flying at 100 feet off the ground. I could make out Icabod standing next to the car. I waved and then pulled the tow release. The Cub shot forward. I cranked it left into a tight circuit.

"Charlie Uniform Bravo is cleared to land Runway 24," the controller said, "wind calm."

"Uniform Bravo."

I landed just short of the intersection and turned onto the taxiway.

"Charlie Uniform Bravo is cleared to the ramp. Call the tower as soon as you get in."

I was expecting the last part. I would have called him anyway to find out what was going on. "Uniform Bravo."

I telephoned the control tower from our office.

"Tower here."

"Hi, John. What's up?"

"Someone dropped an advertising banner on the concert at Buffalo Stadium. The American authorities think it was you."

"Oh, oh. Was anyone hurt?"

"I don't know. You'd better check your banner and then call them. I'll give you the number."

"I'm ready to copy."

I pushed the Cub away while waiting for Icabod to return with the banner. It didn't take him long. The Volkswagen jerked to a stop beside the hangar. The rolled-up message and pick-up poles were sticking out of the passenger window.

"Hi Icabod, thanks for staying."

"I went home for dinner and came back," he mumbled shyly, "in case you needed help in the dark."

Icabod didn't have a driver's licence. He drove my car around the airport in second gear. He must have walked the three miles home and back to retrieve the banner for me in the bug-infested infield.

"Well, thank you. I really appreciate it. Did you notice if the banner was complete?"

He frowned as if he had done something wrong. "I didn't count the letters," he said to my feet, "but the lead mast and tail were still on."

"Good enough," I said. "I have to make a phone call. If you put the equipment away for me, I'll give you a ride home when I'm done."

"Yes, sir."

"FAA Response Line, Inspector Dodd speaking."

"Inspector Dodd, I'm the pilot of the Canadian Super Cub who was towing an advertising banner around Buffalo Stadium this evening."

"Are you aware that you dropped your banner on the stadium parking lot?"

"No," I replied trying to sound calm and controlled, " but I am aware that none of my banner fell off and that the complete message is rolled up and in our hangar. I'm also aware that there was a Cessna 172 also towing a banner over the concert."

The man asked for information about me, the Cub and our air service. I answered each question.

"What else can you tell me about the Cessna?" he asked.

"Nothing," I replied. "I didn't see the registration and couldn't read the banner."

"Uh huh."

"Now what happens?" I asked.

"I just take the information, sir. Thank you for your cooperation."

Great! I said to myself. Now I'll be on pins and needles until we hear from someone else.

I called Henry at home and told him the situation.

"Well, we'll wait and see what happens next," he replied.

On Sunday, the Buffalo media reported that a Canadian airplane advertising for Buffalo Cadillac dropped a banner on the concert at the stadium. That seemed to make it fact. The good news was that the errant message had landed in the parking lot and had not hurt anyone.

I arrived at work mid-morning after a restless night. I was scheduled to tow banners over Niagara Falls. Henry said that he had heard about the incident from several people but nobody had contacted us from either government.

"Tow your banners and don't worry about it," he said.

I called Circus Ground Control to taxi for my first pick-up.

"Sierra Charlie Uniform Bravo, Circus Ground, Runway 24, wind 230, five to ten, altimeter 29.94. Cleared to taxi Charlie, Bravo."

"Charlie Uniform Bravo."

"Where are you going to drop this one?" the controller asked.

"On your head," I replied.

I flew three banners without incident.

One of our first calls on Monday morning was from Buffalo Cadillac. The owner spoke to Leanne. "That aerial ad worked great!" he whooped. "This place is going crazy!"

"I'm glad to hear that," Leanne replied.

"Yah! Too bad it fell on a customer's Cadillac. We'll have a repair estimate for your insurance company by this afternoon."

Leanne explained to him that it was not our banner that dropped.

"Yes it was," he replied. "It was in all the news."

Inspector Kennedy walked into our office at ten o'clock. Henry and I were both there.

The stone-faced, older man fixed his grim stare on me. "So your trouble-making has gone international," he declared.

"Good morning, sir," I replied.

"What can we do for you, inspector?" Henry asked politely.

Kennedy looked at Henry and then back at me. "Tell me why I should not shut down this entire operation?"

Henry had a knack for handling bureaucrats but I was determined to take care of this myself. "Tell us why you would?" I replied.

"I'll ask the questions!" he snapped. "The FAA has authorized me to investigate your activity in their airspace. Show me your Operating Certificate for Aerial Advertising in the United States."

"We don't need one," I replied firmly, "and you already know we don't have one."

Henry had a student waiting. "If I'm not needed, I'll leave you gentleman to it."

"Thank you," I said to him.

Kennedy continued grilling me. "Do you deny towing a banner in American airspace last Saturday evening?" he demanded.

"No sir."

"You flew over the stadium in Buffalo, New York?"

"I flew around the stadium towing a banner."

"Where is that banner now?" he asked knowingly.

"In our hangar. Would you like to see it?" I moved to leave the office.

Kennedy held up his hand in front of me. "Don't bother. You could

I was determined to handle this bureaucrat myself.

have made another. So you deny losing the banner during that flight."

"Yes, sir."

"Show me your company daily flight log for last Saturday and the Aircraft Journey Log for the airplane you were flying."

Leanne stood up from her desk and handed me the documents. I held them out to Kennedy.

The sour man glanced at them. "I'll be taking these with me," he declared.

"Yes, sir."

"Let me know if you change your story," he said. He turned to leave.

"There was another aircraft towing banners during the concert," I said.

"We'll see about that."

I smiled to myself. "Yes, sir. Let us know if there is anything else we can do to help."

He looked back to see if I was being sarcastic. I kept a straight face. He nodded toward Leanne and left.

We held our breath until Kennedy closed the door and cleared the steps.

"Do you suppose that man is married?" Leanne asked.

"To what?" I replied.

Henry, Leanne and I spent the next day and a half speculating on what further action might be taken by either government.

"I still think the worst they'll do is ask us not to tow over Buffalo," Henry said.

"You didn't hear Kennedy after you left," I replied. "He was like a bear looking to nail somebody."

"I wouldn't worry about it."

"You weren't flying the airplane."

On Tuesday afternoon I received a telephone call from Kevin Donaldson, the Chief of Aviation Standards for the region. He was Inspector Kennedy's boss. I had met Donaldson a couple of times. He was everything that Kennedy was not: intelligent, open-minded, friendly, helpful and fair.

"I've been talking to my FAA counterpart across the border," he said.

"Yes, sir."

"They found out that an American private pilot flying a Cessna dropped the banner in the stadium parking lot last Saturday evening."

"Inspector Kennedy will be disappointed, sir."

"Inspector Kennedy's visit to The Flying Circus yesterday was a routine procedure following an aviation incident," Donaldson replied firmly. "He was acting on my orders as a courtesy to the American government."

"Yes, sir, of course."

"The American pilot is being charged with conducting an illegal commercial operation, low flying over an assembly of persons and creating a hazard to persons and property on the ground."

"Yes, sir." I was hoping that was it. "Thanks for letting us know."

It wasn't.

"Regarding this business of cross-border flying on domestic operating authorities."

"Yes, sir."

"There are no Canadian or American regulations that specifically prohibit domestic carriers in either country from conducting sightseeing or aerial advertising in each other's airspace."

"I'm glad to hear that, sir."

"Nor are there regulations that allow it."

"Yes, of course, sir."

"It appears that the Niagara River is the only place along the U.S.-Canadian border where there is a need for such regulations."

"Yes, sir. I understand."

"Good. And the only time the need arose was when you flew a banner over the Buffalo stadium last Saturday."

"Yes, sir."

"So my FAA counterpart and I concluded that there are two ways to solve this little problem."

"Yes, sir."

"We could develop and table a new set of regulations for the next aviation bilateral talks between our countries. This would be expensive and time consuming. It would tie up a number of bureaucrats who have better things to do. It might result in no cross-border flying for any specialty carriers operating on domestic licences."

"Yes, sir."

"Or, The Flying Circus could continue to fly banners and sightseers around Niagara Falls, as could other Canadian and American carriers."

"That would be helpful, sir."

"To avoid another international incident, The Flying Circus could refrain from venturing further inland, like to Buffalo and its stadium."

"Yes, sir. Plan 'B' is an excellent idea. Very well put."

"I thought you might see it that way. We appreciate your cooperation."

"Yes, sir."

Chapter Twenty-two

My place

Iflew home one evening. I didn't do it often. Several things had to fall into place first. The weather had to be good and forecasted to stay that way until morning. The wind had to be from the southwest or calm. I needed to finish work before dark. My old farmhouse had to be stocked with at least 12-hours worth of milk, cereal and dog food so I wouldn't have to stop on the way home. The Super Cub had to be available.

The Super Cub was a necessity because I was no longer married. There was no one to stand at the curve in the country road in front of my place and signal that the coast was clear for a takeoff in a Cherokee. The only semi-level ground on my 10 acres of rolling groundhog pasture was 450 feet of ridge.

The pilot operating handbook for the Cub said it would land and stop in 350 feet. That would be on a paved, level, dry runway in standard conditions and no wind. My experience was that the Cub needed 500 feet of rough pasture to land and stop in most conditions.

When the wind was calm, I landed from south to north. A dip in the rolling land allowed me to glide below the ridge and plop the wheels on the upslope. But the airplane would skip off the groundhog mounds rendering the brakes mostly useless for the first 200 to 300 feet. To avoid hitting the rapidly approaching wire fence at the road, I turned the Cub right and rolled down the side of the ridge to the barn. I parked it there for the night where people driving by couldn't see it.

This particular evening, Summer was working the flight desk. I signed myself out and grabbed the Super Cub's logbook. "I'm going to fly home tonight, Summer," I said. "Henry will lock up."

The university student was sporting a big grin, a very big grin. "I hope you have a wonderful evening," she said in a singsong voice.

"Thanks. You too. Good night."

"Good night."

My place was a 45-minute drive or a 25-minute flight from the Circus Airport. The wind was calm. On arrival I descended over the house, across the ridge and circled for a northbound landing. There was a white MGB sitting in the driveway with its top down. Carol Thomas was the only one who drove that kind of white sports car.

The pretty schoolteacher had given me a ride home when we first met. I immediately began speculating why she would be there now. There is no one in the car, I said to myself, so Carol must be in the house. It was a warming thought.

I braked hard. The tail came up each time the tires touched.

The landing approach had to be "on the numbers" to get stopped on the bumpy ridge. This time it wasn't. I came in high, used up the first 150 feet of stopping distance before I touched down. I dumped the flaps, held the stick back, pulled the mixture control out and braked. I braked so hard that the tail came up each time the bouncing tires touched the ground. I was going too fast. I swerved to miss the fence. The left wingtip dipped as the airplane tipped but it didn't touch. The Cub careened down the side of the ridge and jerked to a stop. I had a close-up view of the barn.

The engine was already off. I could feel my heart pounding and it wasn't for Carol Thomas. I sat in the airplane for a couple of minutes to calm down.

There was no sign of Lady, my German Shepherd dog. She stayed outside all day and always greeted me.

I climbed out and closed up the Cub. I walked around the barn and up the hill to the house. I could see Carol through the screen door working at the kitchen counter. It was a nice sight. The compact schoolteacher was dressed country casual. She looked good. My dog was sitting attentively beside her.

"Your guy will be home soon, Lady," Carol said, "and we'll surprise him with supper."

The dog whimpered.

Carol was cutting up something. "Here you go, girl." She tossed a piece of whatever it was to her. With Lady, there was no chance of food hitting the floor.

I spoke through the screen. "Will you toss me one if I whine?"

Carol screamed. "Eeeekkkkk!!!"

Lady barked. "Arf, arf, arf!"

I opened the door. "It's OK, Lady, it's me!"

Carol clutched at her throat. Her eyes went big as landing lights. She leaned unsteadily against the counter. I had scared her badly.

The dog stopped barking and wagged her tail.

"Ohhhh!" Carol said, trying to catch her breath. "You scared the wits out of me."

I walked over and cautiously slid one arm around her. "I'm sorry."

She cupped her hands over her face and buried them in my shoulder.

I put my other arm around her and held her gently. I could feel her body shaking and her heart pounding. It felt good.

"I guess I should have whistled or something before I hit the porch," I said into her hair.

She looked up at my sheepishly. "I thought Lady and I would hear you drive in."

Her reddened face was smeared with bits of the vegetable she had been slicing. It was also on my shirt. I could have reached for a cloth but

I didn't want to give up the embrace.

"You sure scared us," she said. She looked down at the dog, "Didn't he girl?"

"Woof!"

Carol wiped vegetable bits off her face with the side of one hand. I slowly relaxed my hug.

"Are you going to be OK?" I asked softly.

"I think so." She wiped the other side of her face.

I reached for the cloth by the sink.

"You missed some." She let me dab her forehead.

She brushed her fingers across my soiled shoulder, leaving more bits on my shirt and flicking some on the floor.

"Oh, I'm making a big mess."

"Don't worry about it."

"I guess you're wondering why I'm here," Carol said. Her voice was still trembling slightly.

"I'm glad you're here," I replied quickly. "I'm just sorry that I frightened you."

"Lady and I were going to surprise you with supper but you made it home too quickly."

"How did you know when I was coming home?"

Carol blushed some more. "I called your office. Summer told me when you'd be leaving. I hope you don't mind," she added hurriedly. "You told me your door didn't lock and I wanted to make up for being such a lousy date on the night of the fireworks."

"You must have brought the food. I know you didn't find it here."

She nodded. "I'm making a chicken stir fry. I've seared the meat," she said pointing to the stove. "I was just chopping the vegetables. The chocolate squares are in the fridge."

"Wonderful!" I said. The evening was looking up. "I thought I was coming home to the dog and cereal. I'll feed Lady. Then I only have to set the table for two."

Carol gave me a big, sheepish smile. Her face was still a pretty shade of blushing pink.

Yes! I said to myself, the evening is going to be much better.

We ate in the dining room. The side window looked out onto the yard, the driveway and the barn. Behind it was a red twilight sky.

"After supper, do you want to put the top up on the MG?" I asked. It was the closest I dared come to asking how long she might stay.

She smiled. "No, it'll be fine," she replied, glancing outside. She did a double take. "Where's your car?"

It was my turn to smile. "I didn't drive home; I flew."

Carol looked outside again.

"I parked the Super Cub behind the barn."

She looked at me. "You're pulling my leg."

"No, I'm not."

"People just don't fly back and forth to work."

"This people does. I work at a flying school. Why wouldn't I fly home?"

She stared at me like a schoolteacher looking for a lie. It made my grin wider. "Show me," she said, pushing back her chair.

"No. We'll be eaten alive by mosquitoes out there."

She scooted into the kitchen. "Come on Lady. Where's the airplane?"

Carol opened the back door. The dog bounded out, down the hill and around behind the barn. I could hear her barking when she found the Cub.

I got up and started to make coffee. Carol came back five minutes later madly slapping at mosquitoes.

"I saw it but I don't believe it," she said. "There's no airport here."

"I land along the top of the ridge," I said, pointing to the dim outline of the high ground against the darkening sky.

"It doesn't look big enough."

I smiled. "It's not, but I land there anyway."

Carol took a plate of chocolate squares out of the refrigerator and placed them on the counter. "We'll let these warm for a minute."

We cleared the table together. I poured two cups of coffee, carried them into the living room and got comfortable on the couch. Carol followed with the dessert and sat beside me. She picked a square off the plate and fed it to me.

"Mmmm, this is delicious," I said. It could have tasted like sawdust and I'd have said the same thing but it didn't.

Carol helped herself to one. "Chocolate is my favourite," she said.

"Well, then, you can't be all that bad," I replied.

She smiled and gave me a one-handed shove. I caught her arm and tugged her toward me. She didn't resist. I leaned down, put my other hand behind her neck and gave her a long, full-on-the-lips, chocolate kiss.

"Mmmm," she said when I finally released her. "That's yummy."

She reached both hands behind my head and said, "I think I didn't get it all." She planted a return kiss that was as long and passionate as mine.

"Mmmm, very nice," I crooned.

"Yes, it was." With that, she stood up. "This has been great," she said, "but this country girl is going to be on her way. I'm taking an education course and my class starts at eight a.m. sharp."

"It's not very late," I protested. "Can't you stay a little longer?"

"No, thank you," she smiled, "but I'm glad I came. Supper at your place was a better idea than at mine. Here I can leave while I still can."

128

Chapter Twenty-three

The Motivator

Serge proved to be an excellent salesman but he was hopeless on the instructor course. He did zero homework and fell asleep during my first ground briefing demonstration.

"I've already done this stuff," he complained when I woke him up. It was 9:30 on a Saturday morning, early for the bachelor pilot. "I took the Private and Commercial Pilot Courses, remember?"

"Then brief me on the first Private Pilot lesson." I handed him the chalk and sat down.

He stayed in his chair. "Ahh, come on, it's play acting. I know you know this stuff and you know I know you know."

I wasted nearly an hour trying to motivate Serge. I pleaded, yelled, cajoled and threatened. Nothing worked.

We went flying in a Cherokee. Serge flew from the right seat. I played the student pilot in the left. The young hotshot could fly but he had the attention span of a three-year-old when it came to teaching. I demonstrated a manoeuvre. Serge looked down at the scenery. I asked him to show me the same exercise. He flew around, mumbled a few lines and gave up.

"I can't do this," he moaned. "It's silly. Just book me a flight test. I'll wing it."

"Do you have a minute to talk about Serge?" Summer asked me. It was later that Saturday. There was no one else in the office.

"Certainly."

"I don't want to interfere but I teach swimming and other sports." The medical student paused to measure my reaction.

"I'd welcome all suggestions," I replied.

"Well, some of my students have been those think-they-know-it-all, would-be jocks."

"You mean like Serge?"

She grinned. "Sort of. I have an idea that might motivate him."

"I'm all ears."

"One of the girls at the university is interested in learning how to fly. She is currently training for track and field but she has down time every day. She has been reading my ground school text books."

"I'm with you so far."

"What do you think of Serge teaching her under your supervision?"

"You think he'll respond better with a real student?"

"Not just any student. Ursula is very demanding of herself and her coaches."

I nodded.

"She is not a bad looking girl and is unattached. Serge might rise to the occasion."

"It's worth a try," I said.

"OK. I'll ask her. She might be available for Serge's lesson on Monday."

"Great! Ask her to come early and to be ready for Lesson One."

"I'll let you know what she says."

"By the way; what's her track specialty?"

Summer laughed. "Hurdles."

"Perfect."

Ursula and Summer arrived on bicycles Monday morning a half hour before Serge's 9:30 lesson. They looked like sisters except in height. Both wore Spandex sports tops and matching gym shorts in Circus University colours. Each had medium-long blond hair pulled back into a ponytail. They were both tanned and beautiful in an athletic way. Summer was fit and compact, standing at five foot zero inches high. Ursula was a stunning, well-proportioned and powerful-looking six foot four. That made her four inches taller than me and a good six inches taller than Serge.

Summer introduced us. Ursula gave me a wide smile and a solid handshake.

"Pleased to meet you," I said, trying not to wince.

"My pleasure," she grinned. "I'm looking forward to this."

"Good."

I explained that Serge would be practise teaching with her, on the ground and in the air. "You will not be charged for this," I added. "The experience will count toward your pilot course but you'll also need lessons from a qualified instructor and some solo flying to obtain a licence."

"I understand," she replied. "I studied the flying exercise book again last night."

"How far did you get?" I asked.

"I read all of it. I have some questions."

I glanced at Summer. She gave me an 'I told you' smile.

"Well, Ursula, today we'll stick to Lesson One. Please understand that you are better prepared than Serge."

"Great! I love guys who make me look good," she grinned.

Serge breezed into the office ten minutes late. "Hi, everyone," he said. "Sorry, I was delayed. The cab didn't come to pick me up on time." He headed straight for the coffeemaker without really focusing on who was in the room. "Anyone else for coffee?" he asked, waving the pot.

Serge's exploded hair, puffy face and rumpled clothes indicated that he was only minutes from his bed.

"No, thanks," I replied.

I was standing by the blackboard at the end of the room. Ursula and Summer were sitting at a table in front of me. Serge poured himself a cup, adding two sugars and a slug of artificial creamer. He walked toward us trying to sip coffee without spilling any on his wrinkled silk shirt.

"Oh, hi Summer," Serge said when he spotted the two girls.

"Good morning," Summer replied. She stood up. "Serge, I'd like you to meet a friend from the Sports Medicine College. This is Ursula van Dyke."

Ursula smiled at the sleepy pilot. She waited while he gingerly placed his dripping coffee cup on the table. He wiped his hand on his pants and then extended it. Ursula unfolded herself from the chair. He leaned back as the larger-than-life, well-muscled athlete reached her full height.

"Pleased to meet you," Ursula said, accepting the handshake.

Serge winced. "Ouch... ah, yah," he mumbled, pulling his hand away.

"Ursula is interested in learning to fly," I said to Serge. "She has agreed to let you practise your teaching on her under my supervision."

Ursula nodded and said, "I'm ready to start."

Serge gave me his best unhappy look. "Ahh... and you're demonstrating the lesson first?" he asked me. He reached for his coffee.

"No," I replied. "I did that on Saturday."

"Well... ahhh..."

"Just wing it, Serge," I said, tossing him the chalk.

I sat down. So did Ursula.

"I'm heading back to town," Summer announced. "You all have fun."

"See you later, Summer," Ursula replied.

"Thanks for your help, Summer," I said.

Serge stared at the floor, no doubt searching for divine intervention. He looked up. We were both watching him.

"Ahh... so, let me see..."

A "clicking" noise came from under the table. It jogged Serge into action.

"So, Ursula, are you staying in one of the university dorms?" he asked. The "clicking" stopped.

"Yes," she smiled, "Athlete House."

Serge's face brightened. "Then we're neighbours. I live in Friendly House, the coed dorm."

"Oh yes, across the common. What course are you in?"

"Ahh, I'm not really in a course," he replied. "My girlfriend was a student but she graduated and I'm just staying on in her room."

A sudden realization crossed Ursula's face. "Are you the guy the cab comes for?"

"Ahh... yah, sometimes."

I held my hands together in a 'time out' signal. "I think that's enough for introductions," I said. "Can we get on with a flying lesson?"

"Ah, sure boss," Serge said. "Lemme see... where to start? I guess what we can do is..."

The "clicking" started under the table again. "Ursula, have you flown in an airplane before?" Serge asked.

The noise stopped.

"Yes, many times but only in airliners," the big blond replied. "I fly to track and field meets often."

"Oh, cool. Are you a competitor?"

"Yes, I run hurdles," she said.

"Wow. At what level?"

I cut off her reply. "Serge, the lesson; stick to the lesson."

He wrinkled his brow. "OK, boss." He looked around and spotted the model airplane used for briefings. He picked it up, pulled a chair over and sat down beside Ursula. "Can you name the control surfaces on this airplane?" he asked, placing the model on the table in front of her.

"Yes," she replied with a smile. She quickly walked her fingers around the miniature Cessna 172. "Ailerons, flaps, elevators and rudder."

"Very good." Serge looked happy that the lesson was rolling. "Can you tell me the movements that are produced or controlled by each surface?"

Ursula's fingers danced across the model again. "Rolling, pitching and yawing. The flaps add lift and drag."

"Excellent."

And so it went. Serge asked questions. Ursula answered. Serge added compliments. At one point, Serge bogged down. The "clicking" started again. I looked under the table. The noise was Ursula unconsciously tapping one of her bicycle shoes on the floor. It made a metallic "click" much like a metronome. The longer Serge stalled, the faster she tapped. The pace accelerated until he got back up to speed, her speed.

I didn't say anything about it.

They settled into the lesson. Ursula was keen to learn and Serge was thankful that she knew and understood most of the material.

The student teacher was a long way from the instructor standard, I thought, but at least he was teaching.

Serge stuck to the lesson so I didn't interrupt again until he was finished. "Since you're flying a Cherokee, Serge, can you explain the difference between the elevators and a stabilator?"

Ursula beat him to it. "The Piper has a stabilator which is a combination horizontal stabilizer and elevator, yes?"

"That's correct," Serge said, looking at me triumphantly.

"But I don't understand how it could work," Ursula added.

The smile dropped off Serge's face. I didn't offer to bail him out.

"Well... Ursula," he sputtered. "We'll cover that in an upcoming lesson. Are you ready to go flying?"

"Yes, I'd like that."

I supervised Serge's walkaround introduction. Ursula happily identified the parts and their functions on the real airplane. Serge spent extra time showing her the antennae and landing gear underneath the Cherokee which required Ursula to bend over and stretch out her legs.

"Serge, let's go flying," I said.

"Ah, yah, sure."

Ursula folded herself through the door on the right side of the cockpit. She rolled the left front seat all the way back and slid into it.

I was the next on the wingwalk. I reached in, folded the right seat forward and climbed into the back. There was no legroom behind Ursula so I sat sideways with my feet on the other rear seat. Serge flipped back the right seat and lowered himself into it. We were cozy. To move the control wheel and the rudder pedals, Ursula had to tip her seat back and hold her knees wide apart. She looked like she was ready to deliver a baby.

I coached Serge through an introductory flight, cautioning him to keep the lesson moving. "The airplane is booked again in less than an hour," I said.

Serge was in no hurry. He was enjoying the long arms and legs that Ursula was displaying. "Sure, boss," he replied.

We had time to fly some basic manoeuvres over to the university and back. Ursula and Serge were all grins. She quickly mastered the light touch necessary on the controls.

"You catch on fast, Ursula," Serge declared. "You're a natural pilot."

"You're a good teacher," she replied.

Back on the ground, we debriefed and agreed to meet at the same time the next morning and every morning that week.

"Will you be on time tomorrow?" Ursula asked Serge.

"Absolutely!" the pumped-up bachelor replied.

"I'll see you then."

133

Serge watched Ursula stretch out her long legs to see under the airplane.

She left.

"Nice girl," I said.

"Yes, she certainly is," Serge replied, letting out a long breath. He was watching Ursula pedal out of the parking lot. "All of her."

"And smart," I added.

Serge looked at me. "For sure. I guess I've got homework to do if I'm going to stay ahead of her."

"That was the idea."

Serge arrived early for his lesson the next morning. He didn't have a choice.

Summer also lived in the athletic dorm. She teamed up with Ursula and crashed Serge's pad after their morning workouts. Their victim woke up to find Ursula on top of him, pinning him to the bed while Summer spooned yogurt into his mouth. It was eight o'clock.

"We're teaching him to eat healthy," Summer explained later.

"Healthy? I could have choked to death!" Serge complained.

They told us how they hauled him out of bed, found him still dressed from the night before, carried him down the stairs and outside where they had an extra bicycle.

"I was poisoned and abducted," Serge said.

Summer said that she held him on the borrowed bicycle from one side. Ursula held him from the other. They towed him to the airport.

"I was trapped between the Amazon and her muscle-bound shadow," Serge said. "They wouldn't even stop for coffee. I thought I was going to die."

They arrived ten minutes early.

Serge didn't look any worse than he did every morning. He was protesting but not seriously. It was obvious that he enjoyed the attention, rough as it was.

"I was going to study for this lesson," Serge said, "but they didn't give me time."

"I guess you'll be winging it again," I replied.

He did.

Chapter Twenty-four

Robot

"What do you think of Icabod flying the Super Cub?" Henry asked me.

"Didn't you say the kid flies by the book?"

"Yes, like a robot."

"The Super Cub is not a book-flying airplane," I said. "He'll have trouble with it."

Henry and I were having one of our 'corporate meetings' in the hangar. We were servicing the aircraft at the end of the day. I was cleaning bugs off windshields and leading edges. Henry was adding oil to the engines.

"I agree," Henry replied, "but I was thinking of switching him to the Cub on his instructor course. It's our most available airplane. It would free up a Cherokee."

"It'll make the course harder for him."

"Yes, but I don't think it's too late. He still has dual and solo to cover."

"We really need Icabod to get that instructor rating," I said.

"Well, that's the thing. Right now, he's teaching like a parrot. He mimics what I say and do. I'm training a flying instructor with tunnel vision. Any inspector could pull him off track during his flight test and he'd be lost. I thought the Super Cub might expand his experience."

"Oh, it'll do that all right; like learning to swim in the deep end. He'll fly smarter or die trying."

"Well, I need something to kick-start the kid into thinking for himself."

"What does he say about it?"

"Oh, he's all for it. Doing the banner groundwork has made him keen to fly the Cub. He'd love to tow banners."

"I can't see a robot pilot doing that," I replied.

"You might be right but I think he could fly the airplane with the right coaching."

"Well then, try him on it. See what happens."

"OK," Henry smiled. "I'm booked solid all week but I noticed you have a cancellation tomorrow. If you start his checkout, then I'll switch him to the Cub on his course."

"Why didn't I see that one coming?"

He laughed. "You'd do it even if you had."

Icabod had gone to college, studied hard and graduated with a Commercial Pilot Licence. That qualified him to fly small airplanes for hire. He now considered himself employable as a professional pilot. He wasn't. College had proven that he was trainable but he didn't have the experience to apply what he had learned. It would be hard to show him that in one checkout.

Icabod memorized the Super Cub Operating Handbook. He sat in the cockpit locating the controls, switches and gauges prior to his lesson with me. He knew the airplane had the same components as a Cherokee but in different places: a wing, tail, engine, propeller, controls, instruments, three wheels and other similar ingredients.

The youngster didn't know that comparing Cherokees to Cubs was like comparing a family car to a one-horse open sleigh. Nor would he understand that this airplane was about to hand him his first big setback in aviation. The Cub was more versatile than anything he had flown but it came with the price of being more difficult to fly. I didn't waste time trying to tell him.

"This airplane was designed a long time ago," I said to Icabod. We were standing on the ramp beside the Super Cub.

"Yes, sir. I read the operating manual. This one was built in 1978."

"Right, but the design comes from the early 1930s."

"Yes, sir," he answered politely.

"In those days, tailwheels were considered better because..."

"They were less complicated, more streamlined and weighed less," he said.

"...correct."

It was good to see that Icabod had gained the self-confidence to speak without being asked something.

"So airplanes with a nosewheel are more complicated, less streamlined and heavier?" he asked.

I was discovering that Icabod had a mind of his own. So was he.

"Yes, but they're easier to taxi, take off and land."

"So airliners have nosewheels to make them easier to operate?"

The question made me smile. To Icabod, airline pilots had to be the best in the world.

"Partly," I replied, "but other advantages make the complexity and weight of the nosewheel less significant on large airplanes."

"Why don't we use a Cherokee for aerial advertising?"

"Because we need the Super Cub's high power-to-weight ratio and its long wing to tow the large-sized banners."

He frowned but didn't say anything. At least the kid had been thinking, I mused, but he should be using his college training to figure out answers.

I continued. "Taking off in a taildragger is simply a matter of lifting the tail into a level attitude and then departing the same way you do in a Cherokee or other tricycle-geared airplane."

"Yes, sir," he said.

I pointed to the main tires. "Landing is different. See how the main wheels are ahead of the centre of gravity?"

"Yes, sir."

"When you touch the runway, this type of airplane will bounce its nose up." I used my hand like an airplane to demonstrate. "If the wings are not stalled, the increased angle of attack lifts the airplane back into the air. There it stalls and drops harder. So I'm going to teach you to land this airplane in a stall."

"Why don't we just put a nosewheel on it?"

It was a good question but I didn't want to use up the lesson answering it to the satisfaction of his robotic brain.

"Because we don't have time," I replied.

Icabod frowned.

"Now look back here," I said. "Notice that the tailwheel is connected to the rudder cable with springs."

"Yes, sir."

"When taxiing, we steer with the rudder pedals, like on the Cherokee but it only gives the tailwheel a tendency to turn. It takes some getting used to."

"Why aren't the rudder cables connected directly to the tailwheel?"

It was another good question, with a long answer.

"We don't have time for that either. Let's go flying."

His frown deepened. "Yes, sir," he replied.

It took Icabod 20 minutes to start the Cub, taxi out to the runway and get ready for takeoff. Each step on the pre-start checklist required him to dismiss what he knew about other aircraft, find the item in the Cub, remember how it worked and what it did, and then check it or set it. I tolerated his slowness because he was doing it his way.

His first setback came with taxiing. Icabod added power and pressed his right rudder pedal to turn us onto the taxiway.

"Push it all the way," I said. I was following him on my pedals in the back seat.

He did. The Cub turned slowly.

"Now push on the left rudder pedal," I said. We were halfway through the turn.

Icabod pushed. Nothing changed. The Cub continued to turn right.

"You have to relax on the right pedal to push the left one," I said.

He did but it was too little too late. We turned too far. The right tire dropped into the grass off the side of the narrow taxiway. The Cub tilted to the right. Icabod pulled the power to idle. We stopped.

In a Cherokee we would have had to shut the engine down, climb out and push the airplane back onto the taxiway to avoid damaging the propeller.

"Keep the stick back," I said, "hold left rudder, add power and drive us onto the asphalt."

He turned his head to see if I was serious.

"The propeller clearance is higher in a tailwheel airplane," I explained. "Trust me."

He gingerly advanced the throttle. Nothing happened.

"More."

Nothing.

"More."

The Cub moved.

"Now let go of the left pedal, push the right one and throttle back."

The airplane rolled onto the taxiway in a left turn but the next three things I had told him to do were two too many. Icabod let go of the left pedal. The Cub gained speed going across the hard surface. It waddled into the grass on the other side. I cut the power and hit the brakes.

The kid's neck turned red below his funny haircut. He twisted around in his seat and frowned at me. It was as if my instructions had caused him to manoeuvre so badly. Somehow, I had to get him thinking ahead for himself.

I smiled. "Practice makes perfect, Icabod. Now tell me the steps for getting back onto the taxiway and staying there."

He looked down at the controls and muttered. The Cub sat idling beside the taxiway. Then he mumbled through what he thought should be done. "I push right rudder and add power. When the airplane gets on the taxiway, I push left rudder and throttle back?"

"That's correct," I said. "When the airplane starts turning is the time to counteract the turn, not when the turn is finished. You have to anticipate it. When the airplane stops turning one way, you have to push the opposite rudder pedal to stop it from continuing into a turn the other way. Ready?"

"Yes, sir."

This time he added enough throttle, turned the Cub onto the taxiway and counteracted the turn with opposite rudder pedal. He held the stick back but forgot to reduce the power. The Super Cub accelerated along the asphalt. Icabod stabbed alternating rudder pedals to keep us on the taxiway but forgot what to do next. We zigzagged toward the active runway. I cut the power for him. We stopped.

"Good," I lied. "Now turn us into the wind for the pre-take-off check."

He did.

"OK, Icabod, the challenge on the takeoff is the increasing control response as the airplane accelerates. Start by using lots of rudder to stay straight. Once the tail comes up, stab and release each rudder pedal as needed. Just before liftoff, only press on each pedal as needed."

"Yes, sir."

Icabod called the control tower and was cleared for takeoff. He manoeuvred us onto the runway and applied full throttle. The airplane accelerated and swung left. He pushed right rudder but he was slow moving the stick forward. The powerful, nose high Cub obediently staggered into the air at 40 mph.

"Nose level!" I barked.

Icabod pushed on the stick but got little response at the low speed.

I leaned my weight ahead to prevent a stall. "Stick forward!" I yelled.

"It is!" he yelled back.

I shoved on my stick. "More!"

He pushed harder. The Cub's nose started down. Then the right wing dipped slightly. Icabod moved the stick left. The right aileron went down creating extra drag at the low speed. The nose swung right. Icabod counteracted with more left stick. This produced more yawing of the nose to the right. I pushed my left rudder pedal. The nose skidded left and the right wing started up. Icabod moved his stick to the centre. The yawing stopped. The airplane settled into a 75-mph climb.

"Reduce the power to 2200 rpm and climb at 60 mph," I said.

"The book says to climb at full power and 75 mph," Icabod replied.

"That's correct but do what I tell you anyway."

His neck turned red again but he throttled back and trimmed the Cub nose up at 60 mph. The high angle of attack in the low-speed climb caused the nose to yaw to the left. The left wing dipped. Icabod picked it up with right stick. Now we were climbing with the right wing down to counteract the nose pointing left.

"Icabod, what is 'P' factor?"

It was the kind of book question that his robotic mind could answer.

"It is the gyroscopic effect produced by the propeller striking the airflow at high angles of attack."

"Stick forward!" I yelled.

"Correct. When does this happen?"

"At high angles of attack."

"When do we encounter high angles of attack?"

"At low speeds."

"Correct. What is the result?"

"Adverse yaw to the left in airplanes with engines rotating clockwise."

"That's correct. How do we counter adverse yaw?"

"With opposite rudder."

"Right again. Why am I asking you this?"

There was a long pause. It was not a book question. The Cub continued to dogtrack in the climb.

"I don't know, sir."

"Well, look around and tell me when you've figured it out."

He couldn't find the problem.

"What is the slip indicator telling you, Icabod?"

He looked at the bubble in the tube at the bottom of the turn and bank instrument.

"That I need right rudder."

"Correct. Be my guest."

The youngster pushed his right pedal. The nose pulled straight. The airplane started to bank right. He moved the stick left and leveled the wings. The airplane flew straight.

"Are you holding right rudder?" I asked.

"Yes, sir."

"Why?"

"To stop the nose from yawing to the left."

"Why does the airplane want to yaw left?"

"'P' factor?"

Bingo, I said to myself. "That's correct," I said to Icabod.

"Why haven't I seen that before?" He sounded irritated

"Because Cherokees and Cessnas don't fly at 60 mph. They fall out of the sky."

"Why didn't my instructors tell us about it?"

"They did. They taught 'P' factor and a bunch of other theory of flight. You learned it. Now the sooner you apply that knowledge beyond the school environment, the sooner you'll become a professional pilot. Some day you might even make a flying instructor."

Silence. The neck went to maximum red.

"You can start now, Icabod. Maintain this climb and turn 90 degrees to the left."

The young pilot looked to the left and eased the stick left. The ailerons deflected and the Cub wings rolled left. The nose skidded to the right. Icabod moved the stick further. The left roll increased. So did the yaw to the right. He held the stick over. Eventually the nose followed the rest of the airplane in a left turn.

He pulled the stick over to the right as we approached 90 degrees to our original heading. The wings rolled toward level. The nose shot further left. We turned 20 degrees too far.

"What happened?" I asked.

Icabod didn't answer. He moved the ailerons and rudder back and forth. The Cub seemed to contradict everything he did.

"I don't know, sir."

"Get the airplane climbing straight again and then start over," I said. "Check the slip indicator when you do. I don't want to hear from you until you can fly into and out of a coordinated turn at 60 mph and can tell me how you do it and why." Now I was sounding irritated.

His neck stayed red and a few trickles of sweat slid down from under his hair but five minutes and several turns later, he had it figured out.

"I need to add rudder in the same direction when I use the ailerons to counteract the adverse yaw produced by aileron drag."

"Excellent!" I replied. "Now you're cooking!" We were approaching 3,500 feet. "OK, let's see you level off here maintaining 60 mph."

Icabod lowered the Cub's nose. The speed increased. He throttled back. The nose dropped. The Cub lost height and gained speed. He jockeyed the power and pitch but the speed and altitude would not stay where he wanted.

"This isn't what I asked for, is it?"

"No, sir."

"I have control."

Icabod had used the normal leveling off procedure for cruise flight: nose level, set the rpm and take whatever speed you get. It didn't work because I'd asked him to peg 60 mph.

"I'm going to give it back to you, but first, figure out how to do what I asked."

I set the Cub back into a 60-mph climb. Two minutes passed.

"I'm not sure, sir," Icabod said.

"Do you have any idea?"

"Yes, sir. I think I..."

"Good. Try it. Level off at 4,000 feet. You have control."

Icabod took over. He gingerly reduced the power and lowered the nose to maintain 60 mph. He worked the rpm up and down until he found the setting that would hold the altitude.

"Very good. Now tell the control tower we are clear of the zone."

Icabod pressed his transmit button. "Circus Tower, Charlie Uniform Bravo is clear of the control zone."

"Charlie Uniform Bravo, roger. What is your altitude?"

"Charlie Uniform Bravo is at 4,000."

"Roger, call returning."

"Charlie Uniform Bravo."

I jumped on him again. "You knew to include your altitude in the call but you forgot, right?"

"Yes, sir."

"As soon as you start thinking ahead for yourself, you won't forget. Now give me a full power climb to 4,500 feet at 65 mph."

The shy kid slowly advanced the throttle and added right rudder. The nose went up. So did the speed. He raised the nose higher to maintain 65 mph. The full power made the climb angle much steeper than normal but he held the speed and kept us more or less straight.

"Can you see where you're going?"

Icabod leaned forward to look ahead.

"No, sir."

"Then you can't see what's coming either, can you?" I barked. "What are you going to do about it?"

Icabod stiffened in his seat. The sweat was now pouring down the back of his neck.

"I don't know what you want me to do, sir."

"I want you to use your head to fly a full power climb at 65 mph without getting us killed by oncoming traffic!"

Icabod stretched further but couldn't see.

"May I turn the airplane, sir?"

Eureka! The lights were coming on. "That's a good idea," I replied.

He banked left and then right to clear the sky ahead. He even remembered to use the rudder to counter the aileron drag.

"That's better," I said. "When you level off, maintain 65 mph."

He did.

"Now give me a descent to 4,000 feet at 65 mph and 1,500 rpm, but think about it first."

After a minute, Icabod did a pre-descent check and then banked the airplane to look for traffic below. He reduced the power to 1,500 rpm. The nose dropped. He adjusted the attitude to give him a 65-mph descent. The Cub slowly yawed and rolled to the right. He started to counter with left stick. I was about to yell at him when he tentatively squeezed the left rudder. The yawing stopped and the wings leveled.

"Very good," I said. "What's causing the yaw to the right?"

"The engine is offset on its mounts, sir."

"Correct. Why?"

"To compensate for the 'P' factor."

"That's right. Now leave the power at 1,500 rpm and give me a full stall and a recovery."

144

"Yes, sir."

Icabod checked the airplane systems again and looked below for traffic. He eased back on the stick. The nose went up. The speed dropped. He kept the airplane straight with rudder. The Cub's nose reached the attitude where a Cherokee or Cessna would have stalled. Nothing happened. We flew along with the nose high and the speed hovering around 50 mph.

"Now what, sir?"

"Are we stalled?"

"I don't think so."

"How do you know?"

"We are not descending?"

"Correct. Now give me a stall."

He pulled harder on the stick. The nose pitched higher. The airspeed needle dropped off the scale. The Cub hung for a moment and then stopped flying. The nose plunged earthward. The sudden lack of gravity made his hair stand up. Icabod stiffened in his seat but he stayed with the airplane. He released his back pressure on the stick. The Cub tucked its nose nearly straight down. Icabod pulled us out of the dive.

"Well done!" I declared. I meant it.

The youngster let out a long breath. "I've never seen a stall like that!" he exclaimed.

"But you followed your training and recovered. Now try one with the power off. Note the nose up attitude at the stall. It will be the same on landing."

He did.

"Good. Head back to the airport. On the way, practise a simulated forced approach."

Icabod turned the Cub toward Circus and reduced the power to idle. He trimmed for a best glide of 75 mph and looked around for a landing field. He found one nearby, set up an approach and started through his emergency checks. We were at 3,500 feet.

The Cub settled slowly. The occasional updraft actually stopped the descent. Icabod completed the checks for an engine failure. It was obvious that we would make the chosen field. We were drifting down through 3,200 feet.

"Could we glide to the airport, Icabod?"

He looked ahead. It was about seven miles away.

"I wouldn't try it in a real situation," he replied. "There are lots of good fields around here."

"That's smart but try it anyway. We can always add power. I'll call the control tower."

"Yes, sir."

"Circus Tower, Super Cub Charlie Uniform Bravo is seven miles southwest, descending out of 3,000 feet, inbound for a landing, request a simulated forced approach to the active runway."

"Charlie Uniform Bravo, Circus Tower, Runway 24, wind 240 at 10 to 15, altimeter 29.96. Simulated forced approach approved subject to traffic. Call entering the left or right downwind."

"Uniform Bravo."

We had a tailwind. The Cub skated over the ground.

"Will we glide further at a lower speed?" Icabod asked.

His lights were definitely coming on. He was thinking for himself.

"Try it," I replied.

He pitched the nose up and slowed the glide speed to 70 mph. The rate of descent decreased. He tried 65 mph. The descent rate stayed the same.

"Should I slow to 60?" he asked.

"You're flying it."

He raised the nose slightly. The airspeed slowly dropped. At 60 mph, the Cub settled into an increased rate of descent. Icabod pitched down to glide at 65.

"Excellent. Now you're flying like a professional."

We entered a left downwind leg for Runway 24 at 1,000 feet indicated. We were 700 feet above the ground.

"Uniform Bravo is on a tight left downwind, 24."

"Charlie Uniform Bravo, in sight, cleared to land Runway 24, wind 250 at 12."

"Uniform Bravo."

"My money says you won't make it," the controller added.

"What do you think, Icabod?" I asked over the intercom.

"I think he's right."

"Where are you looking to touch down?"

"At the end of the run..." he started to say, "but we could land halfway along and save half a mile."

"That's right. You'll make an instructor yet!"

"Get your money out," I said to the controller.

Icabod kept the Cub in tight. He anticipated the drift in the turn toward the runway. We were actually a bit high.

"Sideslip?" Icabod asked.

"Absolutely," I replied.

The kid was on a roll. He added right rudder and left stick in the turn to the runway. The Cub obediently cocked its nose right, tucked its left wing down and dropped like a rock.

Icabod rolled the airplane out of the sideslip.

"Full stall landing?" he asked.

"That's correct."

He pulled the nose up. The Cub floated over the runway. A slight crosswind drifted us to the left. Icabod dipped the right wing and kept the airplane straight with rudder. The right tire touched before the stall. The Cub bounced back up but not very high.

"Just keep flying into the stall and beyond," I said.

He did.

The airplane settled on its right tire and tailwheel together followed by the left tire. We were two thirds down the 5,000-foot runway.

"Keep us straight and increase your crosswind correction," I advised.

He did.

"Now gently on the heel brakes."

Icabod carefully slowed the Cub, turned off the end of the runway and stopped.

"Charlie Uniform Bravo is cleared all the way to the ramp," the controller said. "Nice work."

Icabod pressed his transmit button. "Charlie Uniform Bravo, thanks."

He turned in his seat and gave me a grin. "I like this airplane," he said.

"Good. And if you keep using your head, by the time you taxi back to the ramp, you'll have no trouble handling her on the ground."

I walked into the office behind Icabod. The back of his shirt was soaking wet. Serge was there.

"Hey Iky, what's that Cub like to fly?"

Icabod smiled. "It's a piece of cake, Serge. You're going to love it."

Chapter Twenty-five

New girl

In mid July, Leanne told Henry and me that The Flying Circus was busy enough most evenings to need someone working behind the desk.

"Summer can cover two nights a week. After working here all day, I won't do any," she said.

"OK, find someone," we replied.

That afternoon, Leanne was training another girl at her desk when I came down from a flying lesson. I shouldn't have been surprised but I was. The new girl was a familiar schoolteacher named Carol Thomas. She blushed as soon as she saw me walk in.

"It was Leanne's idea," she explained quickly. "She called me and said she was stuck. I was available. You were not around to ask if it was OK. I came anyway. Here I am."

"Don't worry about him," Leanne interjected. "He's a flying instructor. The pilots around here don't run things, thankfully; we do. Now I'll show you how to make an invoice for this student."

Carol was wearing a schoolteacher dress. It suited her. A happy feeling washed over me as I looked at her. The prospect of spending more time close to her was instantly appealing. The thought of working with her was scary. It couldn't be the best way to advance a romance.

"Good afternoon, ladies," I said calmly. "We were point three hours briefing and one point one hours in the airplane."

I wrote the times on the flight sheet. Leanne helped Carol fill out an invoice.

My student was Doctor Ivan, a local neurosurgeon. He had been struggling to learn how to fly for a long time but his head was too full to absorb the lessons. It was too bad. The doctor could afford the cost but not the time.

"Are you still available next Wednesday afternoon, doctor?"

"Yes, yes," he answered impatiently. He was making another unreadable entry in his logbook.

Carol approached the flight desk with Doctor Ivan's bill. Leanne stood behind her. Carol laid the invoice on the counter and looked the doctor in the eye. She spoke slowly. "You, were, point three, of an hour, in, a, ground briefing, doctor," she said loudly, "and, one point one, on, a dual, flight lesson." She watched for his reaction.

"Yes, yes," he replied.

"Your total amount, is, here," she said, pointing at the bottom. "If, you would sign, here," she continued, she made an 'X' in the middle of the page, "then, I will give you, a copy."

Leanne covered her mouth. I could see her shaking with silent laughter. The doctor made a swirl on the bill with his pen.

"Doctor Ivan," I said, "this is Carol Thomas. She's new here."

"Ah, yes," he replied. He offered her a handshake. She took it. "A pleasure, young lady. Now I must be off."

He left.

Leanne couldn't hold it any longer. Her stifled laughter came out snorting. Carol turned toward her and then back at me with a puzzled look on her face.

"What? What did I do wrong?"

"Nothing," Leanne said as she took a breath between guffaws. "I'm sorry... I... I can't help it. You were speaking to the man like... like he was in Grade 3."

"Oh, I didn't realize," Carol said, blushing again. "Do you suppose he noticed?"

"Probably not," I replied. "I think I'll start teaching him like that. It couldn't hurt."

"That was really stupid of me," Carol moaned.

"Don't worry," Leanne said, recovering. "I did the same thing when I started here. You can't help it when you've been locked up with a bunch of eight-year-olds."

I returned from flying with my next student. Leanne was leaving Carol to work the flight desk on her own for the evening.

"I spent a year in college learning how to teach," Carol moaned. "I've only been here for two hours."

"You'll be fine," Leanne replied. "Ask the guys for help when you need it or call me at home."

It was my day to work late. I flew with students until ten o'clock. Carol was still there when I finished.

"I'm just going to push the airplanes into the hangar," I said to her.

"I'd like to help if I can," she replied, walking around the flight desk.

"It's late Carol," I said. "You don't have to stay. I'm used to doing this on my own."

"I don't want my working here to get in the way of anything."

Her big eyes searched my face. "We haven't had a chance to talk all evening," she said.

"You're right. And I'd appreciate the help." I opened the door for her. "After you."

I hooked a towbar to the nosewheel of a Cherokee. "Push on the propeller by the spinner, like this," I said, "and I'll steer."

She placed both hands on the prop and leaned all her weight into it.

"Whoa, whoa," I said, "not so hard, country girl. The airplanes are not that heavy."

"Sorry," she said.

"That's OK but when we get into the hangar, we have to stop."

We rolled the Cherokee slowly across the ramp.

"What do you think of my working the desk here part-time for the summer?"

"What do you think?" I replied.

She smiled. "I asked you first."

"Yes, but I'm the boss."

"That's not what Leanne told me."

It was my turn to smile. "You got me there. What do you think of the idea after your first day?"

"It's a challenge, but I enjoyed it. It's been a long time since I've worked with adults."

"Well then, let's try it for a while."

"But this is your full-time livelihood," she replied. "I don't want my working here to get in the way of that."

"That's funny. I was hoping it would."

Chapter Twenty-six

A tale of two classes

Henry trained Icabod to teach air law to the ground school class. Icabod had already memorized the aviation regulations in college. Henry hoped that teaching something he knew would help him overcome his shyness.

The classes were held in the office on Monday evenings. That July there were a dozen people enrolled including two of Summer McDay's friends from her church choir plus Ursula and a couple of other university students recruited by Serge.

I came down from flying with a student the first evening Icabod was teaching on his own. The sun was setting, there was no wind and the air was hot and steamy. The office windows and door were open.

I walked in to see three students asleep, heads in hands and sweat dripping off their noses. The rest of the class was fanning themselves with notebooks and smashing mosquitoes with their texts.

I quietly finished with my student at the flight desk. Icabod announced that the class was dismissed. There was a polite stampede out of the office.

Icabod looked up from his notes. "There is one more thing..." he started to say.

The room was empty except for me.

"I think you're too late, Icabod," I said.

I made Serge teach engines and airframes to the ground school class. The party boy knew next to nothing about aircraft systems. I decided that teaching it would force him to learn more. I monitored while he practised on Ursula.

The evening of his first session with the class was another hot and muggy one. I taxied in with a student to find the ground school gathered outside of the office. They were standing around the Cessna 172 on the edge of the ramp. They were drinking pop and beer and listening to Serge

as he pointed out parts on the airplane. The cowlings were off. The engine was running. I couldn't believe it! Serge's back was no more than a foot from the whirling propeller.

I hopped out of the Cherokee and hustled over to the gathering. "Serge!" I shouted over the idling engine. "What are you doing?"

He turned. "Oh, hi boss. I'm showing everyone the engine systems."

"With the engine running?"

"Yah. It was too hot and buggy without it. Come around behind and get some air off the propeller," he grinned. "It's cooler and the mosquitoes won't bother you. Help yourself to a beer from the ice chest," he added. "They're two bucks."

Chapter Twenty-seven

Looped

Icabod flew with Inspector Kennedy on his instructor flight test in the Super Cub.

They crashed.

Most of the flying had been completed. They were returning to the Circus Airport. Kennedy told Icabod to demonstrate a short field landing on the active runway.

The wind was calm. Icabod set up a full flap approach at 65 mph. He did a good, three-point touchdown on the numbers. He was about to apply the brakes when the airplane suddenly swerved right. Icabod countered with left rudder but it wasn't enough. The Cub snapped into a groundloop. The left main gear folded under the fuselage dropping the left wingtip to the asphalt. The airplane swung around and came to rest facing the opposite direction.

Kennedy was in the front seat. Icabod told us that the inspector had the door open as soon as the Cub stopped moving. "He scrambled out and ran to the side of the runway," the youngster said. "The engine was still running. I leaned into the front, shut everything down and climbed out."

The Cub was bent but no one was hurt.

The Circus Airport had a war surplus crash jeep. It was kept in the equipment garage. The vehicle was outfitted with large fire extinguishers, hoses, axes, chains and a giant first aid kit; all painted red and rusted in place. There were no dedicated emergency personnel on the field but Barney Swallow, the airport manager, knew how to run the equipment. Once a year, he demonstrated it to the staff at the Circus Flying Club.

When the Cub groundlooped, the radio monitor in Barney's office came alive with talk of an aircraft disabled on the runway. The elder manager hotfooted to the garage as fast as he could waddle. He opened the electric door, pulled himself into the jeep and stomped on the starter. The six-volt system clicked and groaned but the engine turned. It fired, coughed and ran. Barney pumped the throttle. The revs came up. Smoke billowed out of the back. He popped the clutch.

The jeep kangarooed out of the garage in a series of backfires and jerks leaving a trail of dash and dot tire marks on the apron. Barney flipped on the siren and flashing lights. He hunched over the steering wheel and coaxed the ancient machine to the flying club. Three club staff members ran outside. One jumped into the passenger seat, the other two hopped onto the sides and hung on to the overhead rack. Barney floored the jeep, ground through the gears and headed across the infield toward the lopsided Cub.

The air traffic controller had called the Circus Fire Department and the ambulance service. It was a good thing he did. Barney forgot about a ditch hidden in the grass. The jeep hit it at speed and was launched.

The next scene was like a cartoon starring Huey, Duey and Louey. One of the hangers-on was tossed off when the jeep slammed back to earth. The right seat passenger yelled at Barney to stop and go back. The old manager stomped on the brakes. This catapulted the other hanger-on head over heels into the grass. Barney didn't see him go. He jammed the jeep into reverse, popped the clutch and accelerated rearward. He looked behind but couldn't see the first guy lying on the ground for all the dust. The left tires thumped over both of the man's legs. Barney lost control. The reversing jeep slued into the ditch and flipped over, ejecting both remaining occupants.

Two fire trucks and an ambulance charged up the airport entrance road and swung across the main ramp. The drivers were not in communication with the control tower but they spotted the dust settling over the inverted jeep. They roared off in that direction.

I was flying with a student at the time but Henry was on the ground. The controller in the tower called Leanne and told her about the accident. She yelled for Henry in the hangar. He drove out to the runway in his beat-up, flesh-coloured Ford Pinto. Both Super Cub occupants were standing beside the tilted Cub when he reached it.

He stopped the car and jumped out. "Everyone all right?"

Henry said that they looked OK but nobody answered. It's possible that Icabod was in shock. He was staring at his feet. Inspector Kennedy stood silently with his arms folded and his face locked in its naturally grim state.

Henry walked up to Icabod, put a hand on his shoulder and asked him if he had been hurt. The youngster shook his head back and forth. Henry went over to Kennedy and asked the same thing. He didn't reply; he didn't move his head; didn't even blink. Henry stared at him.

No one ever won a silence contest against my partner.

Kennedy spoke. "If you want to know what happened, talk to the pilot-

155

The next scene was like a cartoon starring Huey, Duey and Louey.

in-command."

"Who is that?" Henry asked.

"You should know that instructor candidates fly as pilot-in-command on their flight test!"

"So you weren't flying the airplane at the time of the crash?"

"Your student was flying," he replied.

He hadn't actually answered the question.

"Are we leaving the airplane here until an accident investigator arrives?" Henry asked him.

"That's up to the pilot-in-command and the aircraft operator."

Henry walked over to the Cub. There was no gas leaking so he turned on the master switch and the radio. "Circus Tower, this is Henry at the Super Cub."

"Roger, Henry," the controller answered. "The emergency crews arrived but they stopped at the infield where the crash jeep turned over."

"I think we're OK here," Henry said. "Has an accident investigator been called?"

"He's on the line now. He's waiting for a preliminary damage and injury report from someone on the scene."

"Patch me through."

"Go ahead."

"This is Henry Rains. I'm the aircraft operator. The pilot-in-command is Icabod Brimsmeade. He was on his initial instructor flight test with Inspector Kennedy. It looks like the Cub groundlooped on a landing. The left main gear is folded under the fuselage and the left wingtip scraped on the runway. There doesn't appear to be any other damage."

"Any injuries?" the investigator asked.

"Brimsmeade says no and Kennedy won't talk."

"Let me speak to Kennedy."

The inspector was listening to the conversation on the cabin speaker from a distance. He walked over. Henry handed him the microphone.

"Kennedy here."

"Inspector, this is Pierre Savoir, the duty investigator. Please fill me in."

"I'd rather not at this time, over."

"What are you talking about? You are a government flying inspector. Tell me what happened."

"No comment."

"I don't know what you're playing at Kennedy but I'll find out," Savoir declared. "Is there any blood on the wreck?"

"I don't believe so."

"Good! Now we're getting somewhere. Are there body parts lying around?"

"No."

"Excellent! Then I'm not driving down there to look at a groundlooped airplane. Have a full report on my desk by noon tomorrow. I'm releasing the airplane to the operator. Let me speak to Rains."

Kennedy passed the microphone to Henry.

"Rains, get Brimsmeade to write a report on the accident as soon as you can and send it to me," Savoir said. "I'm releasing the airplane to you."

"Yes, sir. Thank you."

Henry had rope and a shop creeper, among other things, in the back of the Pinto. He lifted the Cub's left wing while Icabod slid the creeper under the damaged left landing gear. They walked the Cub around and tied it to the Pinto.

"The creeper was overloaded and in distress," Henry told me. "It worked but it was a long, slow ride to the hangar. I had Icabod in the back seat and Kennedy in the front."

"I'm glad I wasn't there," I said.

"I hope Kennedy felt the same. The accident investigator was not the only one put out by his lack of communication."

Henry said that he asked the inspector how the flight test went.

Kennedy snapped out his response. "The candidate failed, of course!"

"What caused his failure?" Henry asked.

"He mishandled a short field landing demonstration."

"What did he do wrong?"

"He crashed!"

Henry had lots of time so he continued to question him.

"It looked like a short landing to me," he said with a straight face. "I couldn't have landed any shorter."

"Crashing is not an acceptable method of landing short!" Kennedy growled.

"Did he fail anything else?" Henry asked.

"I'm not at liberty to discuss it under the circumstances," the inspector replied.

It was Henry's turn to be upset.

"Discussion is what you do following a flight test, inspector! It's how I learn what to review before the candidate's re-test."

Kennedy turned and looked out his window without answering.

"I want a de-briefing and a copy of your flight test report, sir, before you leave." Kennedy didn't reply. "I'm entitled to feedback on my candidate's performance, good and bad. So is he. Your assessment impacts his future. It also reflects on my abilities to teach instructors and my record in the government aviation standards office."

The silent inspector continued to stare out the window. Henry kept talking. "Your assessment of this flight test also reflects on you, your office and the whole process."

The man finally turned and gave Henry a hard look but offered no reply.

"I was certified as a Class I instructor by your office," Henry continued. "I trained this candidate according to your government mandated course. A failure shows weaknesses in the chain: his training, my training, your course and your ability as an examiner."

"Are you threatening me?" Kennedy demanded.

"No, sir, I'm not!" Henry replied. "We all have responsibilities in flight training. I'm making sure that we share them."

Henry said that Kennedy looked away.

"You laid it on pretty thick," I said to Henry. I had never heard him so unhinged.

"You bet. Kennedy's silence told me there might be more to the groundloop than he wanted anyone to know. I figured a damaged airplane should at least earn Icabod a pass. I wasn't finished with him, either. We crept along the runway to within sight of the overturned jeep. I told him that there is more to this incident than a broken airplane. I said there might be injuries among the rescue crew."

"You were really pushing it," I said.

"That's not all. I told him if I didn't get a de-briefing and a failed flight test report immediately, that I'd assume Icabod passed and turn him loose to instruct."

"What did he say?"

"He said, 'That it would be a violation.' I replied that if it was, it would be one in a string of violations."

I shook my head and grimaced. "So are we out of business?"

Henry pushed out his chin. "Not if I can help it."

The emergency crews never made it to the Super Cub. Henry was towing the airplane down the taxiway by the time they had attended to the injured rescuers. We learned later that the four had suffered cuts, bruises and sprains but no life-threatening injuries. The guy Barney had run over would be hobbling for a while but nothing had been broken. Another ambulance arrived and they were all taken to the hospital. The firefighters foamed the jeep for good measure and left.

Henry said that Kennedy marched to his car without saying another word as soon as the Pinto reached The Flying Circus ramp. He drove off.

My partner talked to Icabod and kept him busy moving airplanes to make room for the Cub at the back of the hangar.

I taxied in with my student in time for us to help push the wounded airplane into a corner.

We went into the office. Icabod sat down to write an accident report. I finished with my student. Henry phoned Inspector Kennedy's boss, Kevin Donaldson. He was put through right away. I had another student but Henry gave me the details of the conversation that evening.

"Inspector Donaldson, this is Henry Rains."

"Yes, Henry, I hear you had a problem. I just finished talking to Kennedy."

"I believe we both have a problem, sir."

"Well, let's start working on it. Is your lad OK?"

"Physically, yes; mentally, it will take a while."

"Understood. And the airplane is repairable?"

"Yes, sir."

"Good. Kennedy told me that the airplane groundlooped during a short field landing demonstration."

"Yes, sir, that's what he said to me but he didn't say who caused it."

"Was your man not the pilot-in-command?"

"Yes, sir, he was but he thinks Kennedy stabbed the right brake trying to simulate a student mistake."

"Kennedy did not mention that to me," Donaldson said.

"It will be in Brimsmeade's accident report."

"I'll speak to Kennedy about it."

"Is my candidate now qualified to teach?"

"No, he failed the test. Did Kennedy not tell you?"

"Yes, sir, he did but he declined to explain why and he would not give me a copy of the flight test report."

"I'll send one to you when I receive it in the morning."

"With due respect, sir, I would consider it invalid. Kennedy can score anything he wants before you see it. I won't accept anything that he has not de-briefed me on."

"Well, his assessment will stand," Donaldson replied firmly. "He was in the airplane. You and I were not."

"I'm disappointed. This is not the standard of service we normally receive from your office, sir."

"I'm sorry to hear that. I will be following up on the matter. In the meantime, don't send your man flying with students until he has been properly qualified, understood?"

"Yes, sir. I also have concerns that the accident is not being properly investigated. Right now it's Kennedy's word against my candidate."

"Officially, the accident has been investigated, by telephone. The Safety Board representative said that he talked to you and Kennedy before deciding that inspection by him was not required. He will be writing a report after he reads the written submissions from Kennedy and

Brimsmeade."

"In the meantime, who pays to repair the airplane?"

"You do, as the operator, or your insurance company. If you think that government personnel are somehow responsible, pursue that through the Aviation Enforcement Branch or the civil courts. I'll cooperate any way I can. Anything else?"

"Yes. I'd like to book another flight test for my candidate even though I believe it is unnecessary."

"You may do that as soon as Kennedy submits his flight test report to this office."

"I should have a copy of that now."

"I believe we covered that already. Anything else?"

"No, sir. That's all."

"Thank you for your cooperation."

Things were not looking good at The Flying Circus. We were without the use of the Super Cub. It had been generating good banner towing revenue on the weekends. Our list of flight training customers was growing but we didn't have enough staff to fly with them. Our star instructor candidate would remain unqualified as long as the Cub was laid up. Then he'd require additional training and another flight test. Serge had not finished his instructor course. After Icabod's failure, I ranked Serge's chances of passing below poor.

Things could get worse. Henry's righteous response to Kennedy and his boss might have been justified but I was afraid he had poked a stick into a hornet nest. The government people had the power to come down hard.

The next call Henry made was to Darcy Philips, the chief engineer at Derry Air. His shop at the Derry Airport maintained our aircraft.

"Darcy, it's Henry. The Cub's been groundlooped. We've got a main gear folded under and a scraped wingtip."

"Henry, you guys sure know how to keep me in business," the cocky mechanic said. "Was anyone hurt?"

"No."

"Good. And it was the left gear that buckled, am I right?"

"How do you know?"

"Because I rebuilt the other side this spring. Compare my work to Piper's and who's do you think will fold first? Is the wing bent or just scraped?"

"I don't think it's bent but I haven't striped any fabric to check."

"OK, I'll be there first thing tomorrow morning."

"Are you bringing the salvage trailer?"

"No, I'm going to drive down with the welding gear, tubing and everything else I think I'll need. I'm going to fix it there so I can go on holidays next week."

Henry and I were pulling airplanes out at 08:30 the next morning when Darcy rumbled up to the hangar in his hotrod Fargo pick-up truck. He had his three young sons with him.

"Well, if it isn't my favourite airplane wreckers," Darcy called out.

"Good morning," Henry said. He walked around to the other side of the truck. "Hi, guys," he said to the kids as they tumbled down from the cab.

"You've met Team Philips before," Darcy said to me, climbing out of the driver's seat.

"They were here this spring but we weren't introduced," I replied.

"Hey, team, do you remember the world's worst pilots... I mean daddy's best customers?"

The three tykes looked to be between four and six years old. They walked toward us carrying cartoon lunch pails. They swaggered a bit, just like their dad.

"This is Danny, Darryl and Dick," Darcy said. "Boys, meet Henry and Crash."

"Hi fellas," I said.

"Hi," they replied with varying amounts of distraction.

"We'll move one more airplane out, Darcy," Henry said, "and you can drive right up to the Cub."

"That's OK. I'll leave the truck here. Then I won't lose it if I set fire to the place."

The three boys followed their dad to the back of the hangar, swinging their lunch pails as they went. Henry and I finished readying the aircraft for the day's flying.

Darcy declared the damaged wingtip repairable. "I'll measure her up and check for cracks in the strut forks to be sure," he said, "but it'll be no problem fixing her."

Henry and I held the left wing up while Darcy stacked crates under the fuselage. We were both scheduled for flying lessons. I assumed that we'd be recruiting Leanne to watch the boys while the mechanic worked.

I looked in the hangar while my first student was completing a walka-round inspection on a Cherokee. The Cub's damaged landing gear was off and on the floor. Darcy was working on the wingtip while the two older kids were ripping the fabric from the gear leg. The smallest was running to the truck for tools.

I returned an hour later to see the youngest sitting on the landing gear. He was holding it while his oldest brother was hacksawing through a

"I'm teaching them maintenance so they won't want to be pilots."

damaged tube. The other helper was cutting new fabric along dotted lines. Dad was at the bench grinding the ends of new tubing for the gear.

At the end of my second lesson, Darcy and the three boys were squatting around the gear leg. They were all wearing welding helmets and leather gauntlets. The youngsters were carefully passing around a welding torch. It was lit. Each of them melted some welding rod on the new joints under Darcy's direction.

A few minutes later they trooped into the office for their lunch.

"Wash your hands first," Darcy called out to them.

"It's neat to see the kids working," I said to him.

He grinned. "They've been with me all summer. I'm teaching them maintenance so they won't want to be pilots."

The oldest boy was on a ladder doping the repaired wingtip when I returned from flying with my next student. The two younger ones were painting the landing gear tubing. Darcy was welding a new gear leg attachment onto the Cub's fuselage.

The landing gear was on the airplane by mid-afternoon. Two of the kids were brushing silver dope on its fabric covering. They didn't have to bend over to reach it. The youngest was standing on a crate at the bench helping Darcy replace the tire on the rim.

The Cub was parked on our ramp with its engine running as I was coming in from my next lesson. Henry was in the front seat. Icabod was in the back. It was Icabod's voice on the radio.

"Circus Ground, Super Cub Sierra Charlie Uniform Bravo at The Flying Circus, taxi instructions for circuits."

The Cub looked more clown-like than before. Besides the mix of yellow and blue fabric, the left wingtip and landing gear were painted silver.

My student and I parked beside them and shut down. They taxied out. Darcy's three boys were putting tools away in the back of the pick-up truck. We met their dad in the office filling in the Cub's logbooks. I finished with my student and then sat down across from him.

"How did you make out?" I asked.

"Good," he replied. "We'll know for sure after it flies a couple of circuits." He reached under the table and pulled out a Cub tire. "This is off the right side," he said. He rotated the tire to show me a flat spot through to the chord. "Somebody locked the brake."

"Did Henry see it."

"Oh, yah, but what can you prove? Any way, if everything checks out on this flight, the boys and I will hit the road. I'll paint the silver patches when it's in the shop for the next inspection. What colour do you want?"

"Ahh, yellow? Maybe the whole airplane will get back to yellow."

He grinned. "You guys keep bending it and I'll keep painting it."

Henry and Icabod returned after half an hour of practising short field landings. They reported that the Cub flew straight and the brakes worked fine. Darcy left with Team Philips. Henry phoned Chief Inspector Donaldson.

"Good afternoon, inspector, Henry Rains here. I'm glad I caught you."

"Good afternoon, Rains. I sent you a copy of Kennedy's flight test report on Brimsmeade. In a nutshell, your man failed the short field landing demonstration. Everything else was satisfactory."

"Kennedy indicated to me that there was more to it."

"That's the way it is now. Your man only requires a retest in that exercise."

"The Super Cub has been repaired and flight tested, sir. I flew with Brimsmeade. He demonstrated three good short field landings. I'd like to schedule his retest if I may?"

"You fellows work fast. Let's see. It's Thursday. Would tomorrow morning be too soon?"

"No sir, that would be fine. What time?"

"Tell your man that I will be there at ten o'clock."

"Thank you, sir. I appreciate the quick response."

Friday morning I was briefing a student before Kevin Donaldson arrived. Henry was talking to Icabod, trying to keep his nervousness from sending him running out the door.

Chief Inspector Donaldson had visited The Flying Circus once before. He was middle-aged, medium built and soft looking. He didn't miss much. His eyes and ears constantly focused on the people around him.

"Good morning, Mrs. Rains," he said to Leanne as he walked through the door. He was wearing a light grey suit and carrying a briefcase.

"Good morning," she replied, accepting his handshake over the counter. "Please call me Leanne."

"Of course, Leanne." He turned to Henry and Icabod. "Good morning, Henry. Is this the young man who is going to be a flying instructor?"

"Yes, sir." Henry introduced Icabod.

"I'm pleased to meet you," Donaldson said, shaking the kid's sweaty hand.

"Hello, sir," Icabod replied. He looked at the man's feet.

"Let's grab a table over here to start," Donaldson suggested.

The three men sat down to a briefing table. Henry handed the inspector a revised copy of Icabod's Instructor Application Form showing the additional training.

"Thank you." Donaldson scanned it quickly. "Good," he said. He opened his briefcase and dropped it in. He looked at Icabod. "I'm going to ask you a couple of questions about short field landings. Then we'll go

165

flying so you can demonstrate one to me."

"Yes, sir." He still couldn't look the man in the face.

"What would you do if you were demonstrating a short field landing to a student and just after touchdown, the airplane swerved to the right?"

I chuckled to myself from across the room. The chief inspector was asking Icabod what he'd do if somebody messed up his landing like Kennedy had. You'd whack the guy in the head with the fire extinguisher, I answered to myself.

Icabod looked at Donaldson. "I would apply left rudder."

"Good. What if the airplane continued to the right?"

"I'd apply left brake with left rudder."

"Good. What would happen if you applied too much brake?"

"The airplane would tip on its nose."

"What would cause more damage: the tip-up or a groundloop?"

Icabod looked at Henry and then Donaldson. It was obviously a question that his instructor had not covered. "I don't know, sir."

"Good answer. Now you know what happens during a groundloop. A tipover can be worse, believe me, I've done one. Let's go flying."

Chapter Twenty-eight

"Yes!"

Icabod demonstrated a short field landing to Donaldson in the Super Cub. The inspector did his part by staying off the brakes. He presented Icabod with an Instructor Certificate. "Keep up the good work, young man," he said.

Donaldson shook hands with Henry. "Is there anything else I can do for you right now?" the chief inspector asked.

"No, thank you," Henry answered wisely.

The older man bid everyone a "good day" and left.

Our newest instructor started teaching right away. Icabod had talked his father into trimming his hours from eight to six a day. That got him to the airport by one o'clock during the week. He worked for us full-time on Saturdays and went to church all day Sunday.

Summer McDay's friends had been waiting for us to hire more instructors before starting their flying lessons. Two girls from her church choir and one from the university signed up with Icabod. It was a good match. The girls appreciated that Icabod was a no-nonsense teacher who was patient and calm. They didn't know that he didn't know another way of dealing with his shyness.

Ursula and Summer continued to tag-team Serge Santini, keeping him on track to becoming a flying instructor. Ursula roused him each morning and herded him to the airport. He did ground and air lessons with Ursula and me. Summer met them at the Italian restaurant for lunch. Ursula biked back to the university to train on the hurdles while Summer read Serge's next lesson to him as he ate. He was set free to sell banner towing and everything else during the afternoon. They lured him into their dorm at suppertime with more food. One of them served a healthy meal while the other read to him and asked questions.

By the end of the course the Italian Stallion was healthier, fitter and slightly more knowledgeable. The two girls could have easily passed the flying instructor written exam.

Henry gave Serge a simulated instructor flight test. "It's hard to know what he knows," my partner complained afterward. "He repeatedly tried to change the subject away from flying. He complained that he couldn't teach someone who was already a pilot. I wouldn't want to recommend him for an instructor flight test."

"So what do we do?"

Henry shrugged. "Well, he'll probably never be better than he is now."

He was telling me to book Serge a flight test and let him sink or swim but it was my decision to recommend him or not. The results would be on my instructor record.

I booked him a test.

The girls had Serge up, dressed, fed and out to the airport in time on the appointed morning. They wished him good luck and left. They should have stayed. They would have enjoyed his performance.

Leanne and I were standing looking out the window toward the parking lot. Serge was behind us pacing the floor and gulping coffee. A government K-car arrived. A middle-aged woman stepped out of the driver's side. She retrieved a briefcase from the back seat and walked purposefully toward the office.

"I smell trouble for Serge," Leanne said.

"You're probably right, but he'd be in trouble with any inspector."

I opened the door as the woman approached the steps. "Good morning," I said cheerfully. I introduced myself.

"Yes, I've heard of you," she said. "I'm Ms. Cindy Weaver, a new inspector from the Flight Standards Office."

"Welcome to The Flying Circus, Ms. Weaver."

The woman looked lean and fit. She could have been pretty but she missed the mark. She was dressed in a plain, white blouse, plastic necklace, matching earrings and a dark blue skirt. Her hasty make-up job looked better from a distance. There was a pair of sunglasses implanted on top of shoulder-length, dark hair. Her perfume was strength five on the broadcast scale. There was a big, honking diamond ring on her wedding finger.

I introduced her to Leanne. "This is our receptionist and girl everything, Leanne Rains."

Ms. Weaver frowned momentarily at my description. "Pleased to meet you," she said to Leanne. They shook hands over the counter.

"And this is Sergio Santini," I said, motioning toward a slicked-down, spruced-up version of Serge, "our instructor candidate."

The new inspector covered the half-room distance to Serge in male-size strides. She stuck out her hand. "Mr. Santini, I'm Ms. Cindy Weaver."

Serge clasped her outstretched hand in both of his and held it. "My pleasure, Ms. Weaver," he said smoothly. "Please, call me Serge."

"If you prefer," she said without smiling. "Shall we take a seat at a table and get started?"

Serge gazed into her eyes. "Yes, of course," he said. He motioned toward the back of the room. "After you."

Weaver placed her briefcase on a table by the blackboard. Serge reached around and pulled out a chair for her. She sat down and opened her case.

Serge placed one hand on the back of her chair and the other on the table and leaned toward her. "May I get you a cup of coffee?"

The inspector sized up his closeness and decided not to mention it. "No, thank you," she replied. "Not right now. Do you have your flight instructor application?"

"Yes, of course." Serge stepped toward the flight desk. Leanne handed him the necessary papers. She was wearing a smirk. Serge winked at her before turning around.

He gave the application to Weaver and sat down, pulling his chair close to her. She read the form and placed it in her briefcase. Then she removed a flight test sheet and a clipboard.

"To begin, I'd like you to teach me your ground briefing for Lesson One."

"Of course," Serge replied. He reached for the model airplane on the next table and placed it in front of them. "From the introductory flight that we had together," he said, sounding very professional, "what were the names of the basic controls that I showed you when we walked around the airplane?" He moved the model toward her.

Weaver stared at him for a moment. Serge gave her a big smile. Instructor candidates were supposed to demonstrate what they knew instead of asking the inspector questions. Serge was treating Weaver like a real student. It was the way he had taught Ursula but I didn't expect him to do it on his flight test.

She decided to play along. She skipped a finger over the model and said, "Ailerons, rudder and elevators."

"That's correct." He sounded overly pleased. "I love students who pay attention," he added. "They make excellent pilots." He picked up the model. "Today we'll be using those controls to accomplish different things in the air. Tell me, how do we operate the elevators from inside the airplane?"

"By moving the control wheel in and out."

"That's right! How about the ailerons?"

"Turning the control wheel."

"I love students who pay attention."

"Correct! And the rudder?"

"With the pedals on the floor."

"Excellent. From your reading, what do we call the movement produced by the elevators?" He moved the nose of the model up and down.

Weaver hesitated for a moment. Serge was making her work but she decided to keep going. "The pitching movement."

"Yes!" Serge enthused. "You catch on quickly." He rocked the wings. "And the movement produced by the ailerons?"

"The rolling movement."

"Right! And the rudder?" He pivoted the model's nose back and forth."

"Yawing."

"Correct! You are the best student that I have ever taught!"

It was true but I had to smile at Serge's nerve. Weaver smiled too.

She stopped the lesson and asked Serge to show her a briefing for short and soft field landings and takeoffs. He started out the same way. He asked Weaver questions based on the training that would have come before that. She answered them. Serge complimented her.

My next student arrived. I did a briefing with him and we went flying. Serge and Weaver were relaxing over a coffee when I returned. He was calling her Cindy. She was smiling. Serge was asking her questions about a navigation exercise when I departed with another student. I came back into the office around noon. They weren't there.

Leanne read the question on my face. "Serge talked you-know-who into going to his favourite restaurant for lunch," she said. "She drove."

I shook my head in disbelief. "I almost wish Kennedy had come for his test. Weaver is letting him off too easy."

"She sure is," Leanne replied. "With Kennedy he'd have been dead in the water long ago."

"Too right."

I was flying when Serge and Weaver went flying. I was on the ground when they returned. It was mid-afternoon. Serge held the office door open for the inspector.

"After you, young lady," he crooned.

"Thank you," she replied.

They were both smiling. I stood back from behind the flight desk and smiled too.

The inspector scribbled on her clipboard and looked at me. "Can you join us for the de-briefing?" she asked.

"Yes, thank you."

Serge and I followed her to the back of the room. The happy youngster gave me a big smile and a discreet thumbs-up. We all sat down. Weaver cleared her throat.

"Mr. Santini could make a good instructor," she said to me.

Serge grinned.

"His teaching technique is very accomplished. He is good at involving the student in the lessons, which I like to see."

Serge leaned his chair back. His grin widened.

"But his aviation knowledge is lacking."

The Italian Stallion jerked in surprise. He and the chair went over backward and crashed to the floor. He wiggled beetle-like for a moment. I got up to help him but he rolled over onto his knees before I could.

"Are you all right?" Weaver asked him.

Serge stood up, retrieved his chair and sat down. "What did you say about my knowledge?"

Weaver looked him in the eye. "Your aviation knowledge is lacking."

The now rumpled smoothie frowned. "What do you mean?"

"I answered some of your questions incorrectly," she said. "You told me that I was right. I offered several basic misconceptions which you should have straightened out."

Weaver read the list of incorrect answers and then looked at me. "I'll give you a copy of this flight test report."

"Thank you," I said.

Serge and the rest of us thought he had the inspector eating out of his hand. He stared unhappily at the floor.

"I believe that more dual instruction will not help you, Mr. Santini. You need to learn more aviation background material. I've decided to issue you a short-term instructor certification. It will expire in 90 days. I'll expect to see an improvement on your next test. You will have to correct the basic mistakes I make in my role as a student."

"That is very good of you," I said to Weaver, sincerely. "We plan to hire Serge to teach here. I will supervise his instructing closely."

"That should help," she replied.

Serge scratched his head and looked at the inspector. "May I ask a question?"

"Certainly," she replied.

"Did I pass?"

"Yes, you did," Weaver replied, "conditional on improvement by your next test."

He shot one arm into the air and whooped, "Yes!"

Chapter Twenty-nine

Melville

Melville Passmore's voice boomed over the radio monitor in our office. "Circus Tower, this is TriPacer Charlie Lima Oscar Whiskey November, over?"

Melville was a former student pilot of mine. He flew a Piper TriPacer from a grass strip on his parents' dairy farm. The country boy's loud voice was loudest when transmitting. He didn't trust the radio amplifier to do its job.

The hum of the carrier tone continued after Melville stopped speaking. I could picture him hunched over the microphone. His tongue would be hanging out and his thumb would be pressed firmly on the transmit button while he decided if there was anything more he should say.

The young farmer was a frequent fly-in visitor to the Circus Airport. The controller had heard him before. He waited until the carrier hum clicked off. "TriPacer Charlie Lima Oscar Whiskey November, Circus Tower, good morning."

There was a pause. Melville would be licking his lips and pulling in his tongue before pushing the button.

"TriPacer Charlie Lima Oscar Whiskey November, ten miles southwest inbound for a landing, over; hmmmmm, click."

"Oscar Whiskey November is cleared to a left downwind for Runway 24, wind 220 at 10, altimeter 29.88, call established."

…"Oscar Whiskey November."

I had fifteen minutes before my next student so I stepped outside and waited for Melville. The brightly-coloured TriPacer landed, turned off and headed my way. Melville parked the airplane and burst excitedly out of the right side door.

"Mary Ellen says I can go to Oshkosh!" he shouted as he charged toward me.

"That's great!" I replied, mimicking his enthusiasm.

Melville was short, round and country friendly. He was dressed in coveralls and rubber boats. Mary Ellen was Melville's bride. I had stood up with them at their wedding a few months earlier. Mary Ellen had recently announced that she was pregnant.

"You hafta go with me," Melville declared as he stumbled to a stop in front of me. He smelled like he had come straight from the barn.

"Whoa, hold on a minute, cowboy," I said, thinking on my feet. "I can't take that kind of time off in the summer."

Oshkosh, Wisconsin was home to the world's largest recreational aircraft show held annually at the end of July. I had enjoyed teaching the grubby little farmer to fly but an hour with him in a small airplane was my limit. Some day I wanted to see the big show at Oshkosh but spending that much time with Melville was not my idea of a holiday.

"But you hafta go. If you don't, I can't!"

"Ah, sure you can, Melville," I replied. "The world's best instructor taught you how to fly. A trip like that is just a series of short flights strung together."

Henry walked out of the hangar where he had been working on an airplane. "Hi, Melville," he said.

"Hello," Melville replied. The excitement was draining out of his voice. He turned back to me. "Mary Ellen doesn't want me to go if you don't go with me."

"Melville asked me to fly to Oshkosh with him," I explained to Henry. I looked at the farmer. "How about I talk to Mary Ellen? Maybe I can convince her that you won't have any trouble on your own."

"I'm not convinced," Melville moaned. "The furthest I've flown was on my solo crosscountry. I've never been to the United States and I've never driven much past Derry."

Melville had a point. It would be a good idea if I went with him. My trouble was, I didn't want to.

"I think you should go," Henry said to me. "You haven't had a vacation since we started this business."

Melville was watching for my reaction. I couldn't signal to my partner to back off.

"A holiday would be great but not in the middle of the summer flying season," I said.

"I'm sure Melville could go during the week," Henry said. "Then we wouldn't miss any banner towing. Icabod and Serge are coming along. I can do the aerial photography and charter work. They can cover the flying lessons."

Melville's face brightened. "Sure, I can go any time and we can be back in a few days."

This wasn't going well for me, I thought.

"It won't cost you anything," Melville continued. "I'll pay the gas and

we can tent beside the airplane right on the show grounds. I'll take our family camping gear. My mom and Mary Ellen can load us up with food."

I stalled for time. "Can I let you know, Melville," I said gently, "rather than decide on the spot?"

"All right!" he whooped. "I'll tell Mary Ellen that you're deciding to decide to go." With that, he charged back to the airplane and climbed in.

"Flying to Oshkosh and camping with Melville is not really my idea of a holiday," I said to Henry.

"I figured that but you'll never take time off otherwise. Tell him 'no' if you want, but if we can't do some pleasure flying ourselves, then we're in the wrong business."

I had dinner out with Carol later that week.

"Melville Passmore asked me to fly with him to a major aviation show at Oshkosh, Wisconsin," I said. "It's during the last week in July."

Carol's eyes twinkled. "I know," she said.

"What do you know?"

She smiled. "I know that Melville asked you to go to a big aviation event with him."

"How do you know that?"

Melville had been in Carol's public school class as a youngster. She continued to teach in the same country school.

"Word gets around rural communities. One of the other teachers is a good friend of Mary Ellen's mom."

I shook my head back and forth. "What else do you know?"

"Not much," she grinned. "Melville thinks you will go."

"What do you think?"

She dodged the question. "Melville didn't ask me," she replied.

"I'm not really keen to go," I said.

"I can tell."

"Sheesh. Am I that transparent?"

She put on her teacher straight face to keep from laughing at my response. "Sometimes," she replied. "Why don't you want to go?"

I skipped the stinky farm boy reason and said, "I don't want to take that much time off in the busy summer flying season."

"I understand. How long would you be gone?"

"Three days minimum," I replied, "more if we run into bad weather."

"Is this aviation show something that interests you?"

"Oh, sure. It's the Mecca for recreational aviation."

"What does Henry say?"

"Go."

"So it's up to you."

"I guess it is. What are you doing for the rest of the summer?"

"I'm finishing my course, spending time with friends, playing the piano and working the desk part-time at The Flying Circus."

She wasn't giving me an out. "I'd have to do something with Lady," I said. "She's never been left in a kennel before."

"I'll stay with her," Carol offered quickly. Her face coloured a little. "I'd enjoy a little country living. Lady and I can talk about you while you're gone."

It wasn't fair, I said to myself. Carol had avoided staying with me but, for the dog, she'd move in for days.

"That's kind of you to offer," I replied.

"I'm happy to help and I don't charge to house sit for special friends."

"Well, I'm glad to know I'm your special friend."

"You are but I was thinking of Lady."

Chapter Thirty

Beer?

A Boeing Stearman taxied in and shut down on our ramp. I had never seen the big, red biplane before but the pilot was no stranger. His name was Axel. He came to Canada every summer from Germany and stayed with his uncle, George Heinkle, a Circus area farmer and local pilot.

Henry and I leased our Cessna 172 from George. He was a pleasant, undemanding customer. He warned us about Axel before his nephew's first visit to The Flying Circus.

"Axel flies in Germany and vould like my plane to use vhile here," he said. "A few flights are acceptable but please give him check ride like other customers. Charge his costs against the lease payments."

"We will be happy to take care of your nephew," I had replied.

"No, he vill not make you happy!" George answered quickly. "Axel is the spoiled nephew of my vife. He takes pleasure in being difficult. Understand that Germany has many nice people. This boy is not vun of them."

Uncle George had been mistaken. Axel was more than difficult; he was impossible. He had stormed into our office demanding his uncle's airplane immediately. I tried to deal with him but the young snot threw a Teutonic tantrum when I mentioned a check flight with an instructor. Leanne intervened before I caused an international incident.

The job to check out Axel fell to my more patient partner. Henry cajoled the ham-fisted brat into several flights before sending him on his own.

On this year's trip to Canada, Axel bought a Stearman in Collingwood, Ontario northwest of Toronto. He flew it to Circus and arrived on our ramp in a great, engine-revving flourish.

I walked out of the office to greet the unfamiliar airplane. The pilot hopped out of the open cockpit, peeled off his leather helmet and goggles, and said, "Hey, you like my new plane?"

I liked it a lot when I recognized Axel and found out that he owned the

Stearman. His purchase meant that we didn't have to fight with him over the use of his uncle's Cessna.

Axel proudly declared that he would fly the Stearman around on his holidays before having it crated and shipped home.

The young German had brought a friend with him on this visit. Uli arrived at The Flying Circus from Collingwood in Axel's rented Porsche. He was a round, jolly German who spoke little English.

Uli retrieved a six-pack of cans from the floor of the open sports car as he climbed out. "Beer?" he asked, holding them up.

Axel took one. I declined.

Over the next few days, Uli rode as a front seat witness to Axel's flying inability. His pilot would blast the Stearman from its tie-down spot with a burst of power while Uli shouted a German marching song and waved a beer in time to his music.

I saw one of Axel's landings. It started with multiple bounces followed by tire-screeching swings from one side of the runway to the other. It ended with one almighty groundloop into the grass. Uli thought the thrills were normal flying.

I had told Melville that I would fly with him to Oshkosh. Axel heard about the trip.

"Ve go vit you, ya?" he said to me.

"No, Axel, the Stearman and the TriPacer are not a good match."

"Ve trottle back. It vill save us fuel, ya?"

"No. Melville would be nervous sharing the sky with another airplane."

"Ve vill follow, being out of da vay."

I relented, sort of. I told Axel that we planned to clear U.S. Customs at Port Huron, Michigan, across the river from Sarnia, Ontario and then fly to Hammond Airport in south Chicago. I had an aunt and uncle near Hammond. We were planning to have dinner with them and spend the night.

"You are welcome to fly the same route but not in formation, Axel. My relatives in Chicago will be happy to host you and Uli for the night. The next morning we will fly north to Oshkosh."

"Dis is good."

"Melville and I will be departing from his farm airstrip at eight o'clock Tuesday morning."

"Ya."

I marked the Passmore's airfield on Axel's map. "And tell Uli that there is no beer allowed on the grounds at Oshkosh."

Wing Nuts

I suggested to Melville that the likelihood of Axel hauling himself and Uli to the airport that early in the morning was slim and the chances of him finding the Passmore landing strip were zero.

"We'll leave without them if they don't show up when we're ready to go."

Melville never harboured such negative thoughts but he went along with me. "OK," he said, "if you say so."

I checked the weather on Wednesday morning. A slow moving warm front had spread low ceilings and poor visibilities across southern Ontario overnight. The forecast was for improvement.

"It's marginal VFR in occasional drizzle all the way to Sarnia," the weatherman said. "Stations in Michigan are reporting clearing skies."

I drove to the Passmore farm and parked beside the lean-to hangar on the edge of the strip. Melville was inside removing the aircraft tie-downs. The cows in the next field were lined up at the fence watching him.

"Hi there, captain," I said walking into the hangar. "I see you have a herd of supervisors this morning."

"Hi. I'm just getting her ready to go," he called out from behind the tail. He undid the rear tie-down and hustled around to the front to greet me. "I'm really excited about going!" he said. "I..." He stopped in his tracks. "I... ahh... Is that a life jacket you're wearing?"

"Yes. This is the latest fashion for TriPacer co-pilots," I explained touching the vest.

"I wasn't planning to fly over water?" Melville said.

"That's fine, but I'll wear it for protection, just in case."

"I don't have one," he added.

"You won't need one."

I wasn't wearing the bulky red vest for floatation. My former student pilot was an animated flier. He swung his body around the small cockpit as he looked for landmarks and traffic. His right elbow flogged everything in its path as he stabbed at each instrument that he checked. It was Melville's way of flying safely. I hadn't discouraged it when he was taking lessons but I had never endured long periods of his cockpit jostling. The life jacket was my answer to avoiding body damage.

I changed the subject. "It's minimum VFR here and clearing to the west. Let's stick our nose into it and see how far we get."

"OK."

Melville had loaded the TriPacer the night before. I opened the rear door to throw my small duffel bag inside. The back seat had been removed and the space was crammed full. It had the musty smell of an army surplus store. I could see parts of a camp stove, cooking pans, a lantern, cots, food boxes, rope, an axe, boots and sleeping rolls. Large folds of old can-

180

vas filled the rest of the space to the top. There was no room for my duf-fel.

Melville hovered behind me. "I got space for your bag behind the right seat," he said. "You can reach it in flight."

I stepped back. "Ahh, Melville. Did you check the weight and balance?" I knew the country boy had a unique approach to arithmetic. He measured everything in proportions rather than numbers.

His face assumed a worried look. "Yes," he replied slowly. "There's room for your weight and the bag."

"Can you tell me how you calculated it?"

"Yes," he answered nervously. "I'll show you." He hung his tongue out and led me back to the leading edge of the horizontal stabilizer. He placed a stubby hand on each side of the fuselage and pressed down. Nothing happened.

"There," he said.

I looked at him. "There, what, Melville?"

"If I press down here," he answered slowly, "and she don't sit on her tail, the weight and balance is OK."

I had found that Melville's strange ways of calculating were accurate but this one was new. I didn't relish attempting a takeoff from a 2,500-foot grass strip that ended at hydro wires without verifying that we weren't overloaded or out of balance.

"How do you know that?"

Melville had trouble making eye contact when he thought he had done something wrong. He wasn't looking at me now.

"I experimented," he said quietly.

"Tell me about it."

"Well, I knew how much runway I used taking off by myself..."

"Yes."

"A coupla days ago I did takeoffs with more load each time."

He glanced at me sideways. I nodded for him to go on.

"I stopped when I was getting close to the wires on the climbout."

"So you added camping gear until you were using most of the runway?"

"Not exactly..."

"How, exactly?"

"I took the calves for a ride, three atta time."

"You what?!"

The stubby farmer immediately looked at the ground.

"Melville, tell me that you're kidding."

"No," he said softly.

"Come on Melville. Three cows won't fit in your TriPacer."

"I took heifers," he replied in a low voice, "starting with small ones."

I looked across the runway. The cows pressed against the fence were young. I tried to picture three of them sitting in the airplane.

Melville guessed what I was thinking. "I took out your seat and the back seat," he said. "They like to stand up," he added.

"I suppose that's so they can see out the windows," I said.

Melville nodded his head up and down without looking at me.

I pointed to the cabin. "How would you know that this stuff equals the weight of the calves?"

"I lifted them in and out of the airplane. Then I lifted the baggage."

"Why didn't you take off with increasing amounts of camping gear?"

"Well..."

He didn't want to tell me. I waited.

"The calves like to fly."

I knew Melville was too country honest to lie but it sounded like a tall story.

"What's with pushing down on the TriPacer's tail?" I asked.

Melville licked his lips and pulled in his tongue. "I loaded three large calves for my last takeoff. They crowded into the back before I could tie them to their spots. The airplane tipped on her tail," he said, making a tipping motion with his hand. "I coaxed one calf forward and the plane dropped on her nose."

The tall story was getting taller. Melville glanced at me to see if I was buying his explanation. I wasn't.

"I follow that the airplane tipped back when the balance was too far aft," I said. "How do you know that it's in balance with the one cow forward?"

Melville watched his feet scuff the ground and spoke with his head down. "I departed with the trim in the 'takeoff' setting, up of neutral."

I waited for more information.

"She rotated and lifted off without me touching the elevator control."

Melville was talking about stuff taught in engineering test flying schools. Few pilots knew that the airplane balance had to be in limits to perform like that.

Before I could comment, he added, "We can do the same thing this morning. If she don't rotate on her own by the shed, I'll cut power and stop."

I could have argued with him but I would have been wrong. The kid had it figured out.

"Good enough, Einstein, let's try it."

He lifted his head to see if I meant it. I did. His face split into a grin and his body went into gear.

"I've checked her over," he said, "and she's ready to go. We just hafta pull her out."

I scanned the sky. There was no sign of Axel and Uli. "OK, we are good to go."

Melville grabbed a tow bar from off the wall and hustled around to the front of the TriPacer. I helped him pull the airplane outside.

Melville taxied to the very end of the strip, brushing the right wingtip in the tree branches as he turned the airplane around. He set the trim and completed a pre-takeoff check.

"Ready?" he asked.

"Mooooo!" I replied.

He grinned, hunched forward, applied full throttle and released the brakes. The airplane accelerated slowly. Melville's left hand hovered over the control wheel. His right hand was on the throttle. He talked. "RPM good, keep 'er straight, airspeed coming up, no cows ahead..."

I watched his ritual closely, ready to take over. It wasn't necessary. The TriPacer raised its nose as the shed went by on my side. The mainwheels lifted off. Melville pressed forward on the control wheel so the nose wouldn't pitch up too far. The calves at the fence lifted their heads and watched as we climbed past them and over the hydro wires at the road.

"Well done, captain," I declared. "Turn right when ready and watch for a red biplane."

Melville leveled off just below the lumpy overcast. He leaned and looked right, compressing me against the door. Then he turned the airplane toward Derry Airport.

We planned to fly across the airport to a railway track on the other side that would lead us all the way to Sarnia. I selected the control tower frequency. We had agreed that I would work the communication radio while Melville flew and navigated.

I depressed the microphone button. "Derry Tower, this is TriPacer Charlie Lima Oscar Whiskey November."

"TriPacer Charlie Lima Oscar Whiskey November, Derry Tower, go ahead."

"Oscar Whiskey November departed the Passmore private strip five minutes ago and would like to fly overhead the field at 1,500 feet on a VFR flight to Port Huron, Michigan."

"Oscar Whiskey November, the current Derry weather is below VFR at 800 overcast, five miles in light drizzle and fog, altimeter 29.88."

"Oscar Whiskey November requests Special VFR clearance through the control zone."

"Special VFR is approved, Oscar Whiskey November, continue and report over the airport. I have no other traffic at this time. Your flight plan is being activated."

"Whiskey November, thank you."

Melville continued his monologue. "Level 1,500 feet, check carb heat, trim, crossing that road, engine instruments OK..."

His animation continued too. I sat slightly turned in my seat with my left arm resting on the canvas behind Melville to minimize being pummeled. The life jacket worked. It took up more room but the elbows and body slams were easier to take.

"Derry Tower, Oscar Whiskey November is coming up overhead the field at 1,500 feet."

"Oscar Whiskey November, in sight, call clearing the control zone to the west."

"Whiskey November."

Melville flew, navigated, talked and rocked. I called the tower clear of Derry's five-mile control zone.

"Oscar Whiskey November," the controller replied, "cleared enroute, altimeter 29.89."

"Whiskey November."

Melville found the railroad tracks and turned to follow them. I was about to change to an enroute radio frequency when another aircraft called Derry tower.

"Hazzy-hash, hash-az-haashahaz, hash hash."

I recognized the static-filled transmission immediately. It was Axel in the Stearman. The combination of unshielded ignition, German accent, loud engine and wind in the microphone made him unreadable. The controllers at our home airport were familiar with the airplane, its poor radio and unpredictable pilot. Not at Derry.

"Aircraft calling Derry, your transmission is unreadable. Try another radio and remain clear of the control zone. The Derry weather is 800 overcast, five miles in light drizzle, altimeter 29.89."

Axel didn't have another radio.

"Haz-hash, hash-az-haashahaz, hash hash, hashhhh haasshh!"

The transmission was just as bad but louder.

"Aircraft calling Derry, your transmission is still unreadable. I check you are east of the airport. Remain clear of the control zone, altimeter 29.89."

"That's the German Air Force," I said to Melville. "Keep an eye open for them. They'll be following these same railway tracks."

"OK," Melville replied, swinging around in his seat to look back.

I spotted them 20 minutes later coming from behind on our right side.

"Here they come," I said to Melville. "Hold your course. I'll yell if you need to break left or right."

The only way they could have caught us so quickly was to fly through the Derry Control Zone without permission instead of around it. I kept my face pressed against the right side window and watched the red biplane bob and weave toward us. The airplane caught up and waltzed past. Two

The red biplane rocked like it was flying to German marching music.

figures waved merrily from their cockpits. They continued to fly on and disappeared into the haze ahead.

"Maybe we won't have to worry about them anymore," I suggested hopefully.

The low cloud was with us all the way. We didn't see the Stearman again or hear Axel on any of the frequencies we monitored.

Melville and I landed and cleared U.S. Customs at Port Huron. There was no sign of the Germans. We walked back outside the customs office in time to see a red Stearman wobble out of the sky, bounce on the runway, swerve and then groundloop to a stop in the grass. Axel gunned the engine and taxied across the infield to the ramp. Uli waved a beer can at us.

Melville and I waited until the big, round engine was shut down. Uli immediately jumped out and lit a cigarette. Then he duck-walked around the airplane and started relieving himself on the grass.

The pair was dressed in matching bright red flight suits. I found out later that they were up early because they partied all night instead of going to bed.

The customs officer came out, noted the Canadian registration and approached the rear cockpit. Melville and I were within earshot.

"Where you from?" he asked Axel.

"Germany, da two of us," Axel replied, pointing to Uli at the tail. He held out two passports.

"Where did you depart from this morning?"

"Canada."

"Where are you going?"

"Oshkosh."

Uli walked up beside the officer. He was grinning and puffing on a cigarette.

"Do you have anything that you are leaving in the United States?" the customs man inquired.

"Beer?" Uli replied.

"You have beer?" the man-in-uniform asked.

Uli's face lit up. "Beer!"

"No, no beer, officer," Axel said. "He vants to know if you have beer. He drank his and is tirsty alvays."

"Beer?" Uli asked hopefully.

The customs man scratched his head. "Come inside and we'll complete the paperwork."

Melville and I waited by the TriPacer. I was expecting the worst. As far as I knew, Axel had never filed a transborder flight plan, had not completed any customs forms in advance and did not have papers covering the Stearman's sale and re-registration.

The pair came back out smiling 10 minutes later. Apparently the customs officer considered them one more innocent nuisance among the stream of Canadian aircraft clearing into the United States on the way to Oshkosh that week.

"Ve go now?" Axel asked.

"We are ready," I replied.

"OK."

We departed into improving weather. Axel took off behind us and charged past with Uli waving. The big biplane continued on until it disappeared ahead.

I had marked our destination airport on Axel's map. I expected him to be there when we arrived later that afternoon. He wasn't.

Hammond Airport was a single, privately owned strip of crumbling asphalt wedged into housing projects in suburban south Chicago. The narrow runway stretched between rows of aircraft parked in tie-downs.

Melville flew overhead. The sight of the small airport nestled among buildings made him nervous. He started to hum. "Hummmmmm."

"The runway is the same size as your strip at home," I said. "Pretend the rows of airplanes are cows lined up at the fence."

He looked at me with widening eyes.

"You can do it," I declared.

"HummmMMMM!"

It took lots of humming, tongue hanging, talking and cockpit gyrations, but Melville nailed the landing. He taxied to the fuel pumps on a small ramp at the far end.

The fixed base operator said that he had not seen or heard from the Stearman crew.

"It's just as well," I said to Melville. "There is not enough airport here for one of Axel's arrivals."

I phoned my aunt and uncle. They drove to the airport in the time it took Melville and me to have the TriPacer refueled and tied down. We agreed to go out for dinner nearby and then check back for the wayward Germans. We left a message with the refueler.

There was no sign of the duo when we returned. The sun had set. The runway lights were on. Then I heard a radial engine. The silhouette of an unlit Stearman appeared overhead against the darkening sky. The biplane cranked into a steep turn to the left and joined the circuit. We stood and watched. It disappeared from sight descending on the base leg.

Two long minutes later, we could hear the tires chirp over the popping of the exhaust signaling touchdown one, two and three. The chirps became screeches, as the airplane must have swerved left and right. The Stearman came into view nearing the end of the runway. Axel clamped hard on both brakes. The tail lifted. The big biplane snapped around. It came to rest beside the fuel pumps, facing the other way.

"Bravo!" my uncle cheered. "I have never seen such fantastic flying."

We approached the Stearman to the sound of high volume German being spoken rapidly. Axel spotted us and stopped yelling at Uli.

"Ahh, ve are here?" he called out.

"Yes, you are," I replied.

Uli grinned from the front cockpit. "Beer?"

The story of their flight unfolded back at the same restaurant over dinner and beers for the wayward crew. They had spent the afternoon getting lost and landing for directions at a series of airports around Michigan. They had a merry time until sunset.

Uli had been denied cigarettes in flight because his lighter didn't work in the windy cockpit. As it got dark, he noticed a flame shooting out of the engine exhaust pipe. The pipe ran along the right side of the fuselage and ended below his elbow. The flame had not been visible in daylight.

Uli stuck a cigarette in his mouth, undid his harness, leaned over the side and held his face to the flame. Axel thought he was jumping out. The pair did not have an intercom. Axel threw the Stearman into a steep turn to the left to keep his passenger in the airplane. Uli lit the cigarette and fell back into his seat. This scenario was repeated for several smokes, including overhead the Hammond Airport.

The pair impressed my aunt and uncle with their matching flight suits and their heel clicking, head bowing displays of respect. My uncle toasted the two visitors at the restaurant.

I raised my glass. "Drink up, Uli," I said. "There is no beer allowed at Oshkosh."

"Beer, ya?"

"No beer, Oshkosh."

"No beer?"

The next morning we dragged them out of bed and to the airport. Their eye colour matched their red uniforms. Uli looked the worst. His eyebrows and hair had been singed the day before.

Melville and I departed first. We circled over the airport, wagged our wings at my aunt and uncle and headed north. We watched the Stearman waltz down the runway and stagger into the air. It flew straight out, westbound.

"Unless they turn," I said to Melville, "we don't have to worry about them anymore."

"You've said that before."

We flew low along the shore of Lake Michigan, past downtown Chicago to Oshkosh. We joined the parade of aircraft headed for the right downwind leg of Runway 27. Melville's running dialogue to himself and his cockpit gyrations doubled in speed but he stayed in line. He landed on the designated spot, turned off and followed the paddle wavers to the tie-downs. We were directed to a recently vacated space on the end of a low-numbered row.

"Great flying captain!" I declared.

He grinned and released a breath that he must have been holding for a long time.

We were tying down the TriPacer when Melville pointed to a red Stearman flying overhead. We watched as Axel cut into the line on the right downwind. The airplanes behind the biplane followed its wandering flight path. I held my breath as the Stearman curved around onto final. It bounced a couple of times on the runway, swerved a bit and then ground-looped into the grass about where it was supposed to exit the asphalt anyway.

The ground crew waved their paddles madly toward the vintage aircraft parking area but Axel had spotted Melville's TriPacer. He gunned the engine and charged toward us. Uli grinned and waved. Axel parked his airplane at the end of our row and shut it down.

Several paddle warriors surrounded the Stearman. They told Axel that he couldn't leave it there. He smiled and said, "Ya," many times.

Uli climbed out. "Beer?" he asked.

"No beer, Uli," I said.

"Beer?"

The ground crew found an empty spot nearby where Axel could park. He restarted the engine and moved the airplane. We didn't notice Uli wander off. Melville and I helped Axel tie the Stearman down. When we were done, a red, cut-off Volkswagen driven by EAA President Paul Poberezny drove up between the rows of aircraft. Uli was in the passenger seat.

"Beer!" he shouted, indicating that we should climb into the back seat.

We walked up to the car and introduced ourselves to Paul.

"Your friend here has been asking for beer," Paul said. "I told him there is no alcohol on the grounds at Oshkosh but he insisted on beer, beer, beer!"

"Sorry about that, Paul," I said. "Uli is from a part of Germany where beer is life, sort of like the milk of human kindness. Thanks for bringing him back. We'll keep him out of trouble."

"Well, if he came from Germany to drink with me, then we'll see what we can find. Hop in."

Wing Nuts

We did. Paul drove us to his house behind the main grounds. We followed him into his kitchen. In his refrigerator were four cans of beer. He handed one to each of us. Uli snapped his open with a big smile and held it up.
"Beer!"

Chapter Thirty-one

Looking up

I survived Melville. The happy farmer's contagious enthusiasm made it easy. The aviation show was a recreational pilot's paradise. There were thousands of small aircraft. Melville was excited to see each one. He talked to anyone who would listen and collected bags of brochures. We wore out our legs walking for hours in the heat and collapsed into the stinky Passmore family tent each night.

I saw Axel and Uli twice. They announced that they were staying through the weekend leaving Melville and me on our own for the trip home.

We departed on Friday morning, beat the bad weather and made it all the way back in one day.

I telephoned Carol from our last stop in Sarnia. "I'll be home this evening," I said.

"Did you have fun?"

"Absolutely."

"That's great. Lady and I will be here when you arrive. We miss you."

It was warming news. She missed me and she was waiting for me.

"I'm looking forward to seeing you," I replied.

Melville and I landed at the Passmore farm at seven o'clock that evening. I helped him push the airplane into the shed.

"Thank you for inviting me along, Melville," I said sincerely. "I really enjoyed myself."

"I had the most fun," he declared, pumping my arm vigorously. "Without you, I'da been circling that crazy airport until the cows came home trying to land!"

"We made a good team," I replied.

I drove home.

Carol let Lady out when I pulled into the driveway. The dog bounded across the yard.

"Hi there, girl."

She jumped up, wagged her tail and licked my face. Carol appeared on

Lady planted both front paws on my car door and licked my face.

the side porch. Lady raced back to her.

"I see her allegiance has changed," I called out. I lifted my duffel bag off the back seat.

She smiled. "You're the one who went away."

I headed across the lawn. I had only seen Carol dressed in business or semi-casual clothes. She always looked good to me. I hadn't thought of her looking better. Now she was standing on the porch, smiling. She was wearing her hair brushed back, a light touch of make-up, a plaid shirt with the sleeves rolled up and the neck open and a pair of nicely fitting jeans.

She looked so naturally comfortable and happy that I wanted to throw my arms around her and never let go.

I walked up to the porch. She placed her hands on my shoulders before I stepped up to her level. We were eye to eye and lips to lips.

"Welcome back," she said and then gave me a big kiss.

I dropped my duffel, put both hands around her and held her tight. The embrace would have lasted longer but the dog barked.

Carol jumped and pulled away. "Oops," she exclaimed. "We've both been waiting supper for you."

Lady barked once more.

"Well, let's go," she said to the dog. She opened the door.

The kitchen smelled wonderful.

"I hope you like stew," Carol said. "It's the only thing that gets better the longer it waits."

"It smells great!"

Carol had set aside some stew in the dog bowl to cool. She placed it on the floor. I was thinking that Lady would probably bite me the next time I tried to feed her out of a can.

Carol and I ate together at the kitchen table. She laughed when I told her about Melville excitedly scurrying from airplane to airplane at the aviation show. I chuckled at her description of Serge acting like the king of flying instructors at The Flying Circus.

"There have been a steady stream of new customers," she said.

"Super! Things are looking up."

"I think so."

We cleared the table and did the dishes. Carol finished washing and wiped her hands. She reached up and put her arms around my neck.

"I hope you're not going to run off right away," I said.

Carol smiled. "No, I'm going to finish the kiss we started on the porch and then I'm going to run off."

Before I could protest, she pulled my face to hers and kissed me like she really meant it.

I opened my eyes when she let go. Her face looked very dreamy.

"The night is young," I said, holding on to her.

"I know," she smiled. "So are we. Now I'm going home to my own bed. I plan to have sweet dreams."

"Is this to be continued?" It was a bold question to ask a modest country girl.

"I hope so," she replied.

Lady and I stood on the driveway. Carol tooted and waved as she roared off in her MG. The dog whined for more stew.

I took a cold shower.

Chapter Thirty-two

Above and Beyond

Barry McDay opened the office door. His wife Sally was standing on the sidewalk behind him. She was so pregnant that he had to help her up the three steps into the building. She looked overdue. She was, with twins.

It was mid-afternoon at The Flying Circus. The office was busy. Henry and I were there. Icabod had just come down with a student. Serge was briefing another. Carol had arrived to take over the desk from Leanne.

Sally was introduced. She was a pretty girl with a face puffy with impending double motherhood. Her short blond hair was tucked behind her ears and her body was draped in a tent of a dress.

She returned everyone's greeting with an uncomfortable smile. Room was made for her on the couch. Barry helped her to sit down. She leaned back and rubbed her big belly.

"We came from the doctor's office," Barry announced. "He has scheduled a Cesarean section for tomorrow morning."

"I bet you'll be glad to have it over with," Leanne said to Sally. She was the only one in the room qualified to make that statement. The expectant mother nodded in agreement.

"I read about high altitude birth inducement," Barry continued. "Apparently, the reduced atmospheric pressure helps bring on labour."

Nobody said anything. Images of a messy airborne birth in a small airplane flashed through my mind.

"Is the Cessna available for an hour or so?" Barry asked.

Leanne checked the sheets. "Yes," she replied. "Two hours."

"I thought I'd take Sally as high as we can go and see if we can make something happen."

There was another silence.

Leanne spoke for all of us. "Ah, Barry. If Sally goes into labour up there, you might not get back down in time."

Barry scratched his head. "That's possible but Sally was a nurse."

Leanne jammed her hands on her hips and gave him a stern look.

194

"Men! What if you were the one overdue?"

"Maybe we should take someone with us," Barry said.

The room went quiet again.

Henry took a turn. "Barry, I don't think any of us are qualified to help Sally give birth in the back seat of the Cessna."

"Oh," Barry replied.

I caught Carol's eye. She shook her head back and forth vigorously.

"I am," a voice declared from the other side of the room. It was Icabod. He had been debriefing his student. "I'm a qualified St. Johns Ambulance attendant with midwife training," he said. "I'll go with them."

You could have knocked over any of the staff with a feather. It wasn't that Icabod was trained in first aid that surprised us. It was that he calmly spoke up and volunteered to be a midwife.

"Thanks Icabod," Barry said. "Is that OK with you, Sally?"

"Yes," she grunted firmly. "Anything is better than surgery."

"The ladies at the desk will make your next booking," Icabod said to his student. "I'll see you then." He stood up. "Barry, if you check over the Cessna, I'll put together some things I might need. And take the front passenger seat out of the airplane."

"OK," Barry replied. "We have a clean blanket in the car if you need it. Sally, you wait here for a few minutes." She nodded.

"I'll help you, Barry," Henry said.

"Thanks."

Icabod walked over and lifted the big, metal first aid kit off the office wall. He placed it on a table, opened the lid and began checking each item.

"Is there anything I can do to help?" I asked him.

He looked up from the kit. "Yes," he replied. "Can you find a jug or something to carry hot water and maybe some towels?"

"I'll look."

"There are two empty milk jugs in my car," Leanne offered, "and there are paper towels here." She got up and opened the stores cabinet behind her desk.

"I'll get the jugs," I said.

"I'll get the blanket," Carol offered. "Which car is it?"

"The blue station wagon," Sally replied.

Carol and I walked to the parking lot together. "I think this is a bit crazy," I said to her.

"Me too, but can it do any harm?"

"I suppose not."

"It's kind of exciting. It was fun to see everyone spring into action. Nothing like this ever happens in Grade 3."

Ten minutes later, Sally was installed in the rear seat of the Cessna with Icabod beside her. The first aid kit and water jugs were in the baggage compartment behind them. Barry was in the pilot seat. He fired up the engine and called the Circus Ground Controller. Everyone in the office was listening to the radio monitor.

The controllers knew Barry and his pregnant wife. He had probably talked to them about this flight.

"Circus Ground, Cessna Lima Uniform Foxtrot Tango at the Circus ramp, taxi instructions for a local flight south."

"Cessna Lima Uniform Foxtrot Tango, Runway 24, wind 240 at 5 to 10, altimeter 30.10, taxi Delta, Charlie, Bravo."

"Uniform Foxtrot Tango."

The controller came right back. "Is this the Baby Express?"

"Affirmative," Barry replied. We could hear the grin in his voice.

He called the tower when he was ready to go. "Circus Tower, Uniform Foxtrot Tango is ready for take off, Runway 24."

"Baby Express is cleared for take off Runway 24, wind 240 at 10."

"Baby Express."

Barry radioed again when he was clear of the five-mile control zone. I knew he'd be switching to Toronto Centre, the area radar controller. I changed the frequency on the monitor.

"Toronto Centre, Cessna 172, Lima Uniform Foxtrot Tango, six miles south of the Circus Airport climbing through 2,000 feet, over."

"Cessna Lima Uniform Foxtrot Tango, Toronto, go ahead."

"Lima Uniform Foxtrot Tango is on a VFR local flight. I'd like to climb to 12,500 feet flying between here and Welland and back."

"Uniform Foxtrot Tango, squawk 5551."

"Uniform Foxtrot Tango."

"Uniform Foxtrot Tango, radar contact eight miles south of Circus. I have IFR traffic, a Boeing 727 at your ten o'clock, 15 miles, descending through 6,000 inbound to Toronto. Call reaching 4,000."

"Uniform Foxtrot Tango will call at 4,000."

The Boeing traffic descended out of the way. The Cessna was cleared up to 12,500. It would take them half an hour to get there. We went back to work. Carol promised to keep listening to the office radio.

I went up with a student in a Cherokee on a local flight. I switched to the Toronto Centre frequency and listened in as soon as I cleared the Circus Control Zone.

"Toronto Centre, Cessna Uniform Foxtrot Tango is level at 12,500."

"Uniform Foxtrot Tango, roger, advise any change in altitude."

I taught my lesson with the radio volume low. I could hear airline traffic flying in and out of Toronto but nothing from Barry for half an hour.

"Toronto Centre, Cessna Uniform Foxtrot Tango, is leaving 12,500 for a shuttle descent between Circus and Welland."

"Uniform Foxtrot Tango, I check. I have no immediate traffic for you. Call through 4,000."

"Uniform Foxtrot Tango."

There were no babies crying in the background of Barry's transmissions. His voice carried the disappointment of no results. I continued with my lesson.

"Toronto, Cessna Uniform Foxtrot Tango is through 4,000."

"Uniform Foxtrot Tango, roger. You're 15 miles south of Circus, no further traffic. Radar service is terminated. Squawk 1200 and switch to Circus Tower."

"Uniform Foxtrot Tango, thank you."

I changed the Cherokee's radio over to Circus Tower and finished the lesson.

"Circus Tower, Cessna Lima Uniform Foxtrot Tango is 12 miles south, descending out of 3,800, inbound for landing."

"Cessna Lima Uniform Foxtrot Tango, Circus Tower, Runway 24, wind 240 at 10, altimeter 30.08. I have three VFRs on local flights to the southwest and one in the circuit. Call joining on a left downwind for Runway 24."

"Uniform Foxtrot Tango."

"Do you still have enough seats for all of your passengers, Uniform Foxtrot Tango?"

"Affirmative, unfortunately."

My student called approaching the control zone and was also given a left downwind for 24. I pointed out the Cessna high and to our right.

"Slow down and follow him," I said.

"Circus Tower, Uniform Foxtrot Tango is joining a left downwind 24."

"Uniform Foxtrot Tango, roger, you're number one to a Warrior touching down."

"Uniform Foxtrot Tango."

My student reported joining the circuit behind the Cessna. We were made number two. The Cessna landed and turned off. So did we. We followed them to the ramp and shut down beside them.

I imagined that Barry might have tried steep turns and sharp pull-ups to help Sally go into labour. The gyrations and thin air should have turned the poor girl green. My student and I walked over. I opened the door on the right side of the Cessna.

"Can we help you climb out?" I asked Sally.

"Yes, please," she said cheerfully. She held out both arms.

My student took one and I held the other. "Gently now," I said.

"What a wonderful flight!" Sally exclaimed. "We could see Niagara Falls, Toronto, Derry, both sides of Lake Erie and most of Lake Ontario."

We eased her onto the airplane's step.

"Barry tried every manoeuvre in the book," she declared. "It was better than a roller-coaster."

We helped her onto the ground.

"But no labour pains?" I asked.

"Nothing," Sally replied. Then she lowered her voice. "You better check Icabod. He was so sweet. He kept me calm by talking to me on the way up but he didn't say much when Barry started yanking and banking."

Icabod was pulling the first aid kit out of the baggage compartment. He looked a little green.

Barry walked around to our side. "We tried," he said, "but no cigar, yet."

"I thought Sally would be the worse for wear after a flight like that," I said.

Sally laughed. "I was a nurse working medevac flights when Barry and I met. It was fun to be back in the air and a nice break from waiting for the labour pains."

"Well, too bad it didn't work," I said.

"Ready to go home dear?" Barry asked his wife.

Sally looked at me. "Is there anyone in the office?" she asked.

I checked the parking lot. "Yes. Carol and Leanne are here and our next students."

She looked at Barry. "Can we visit for a while? I feel much better. Everyone has been so nice. All I can do at home is sit around and worry about tomorrow."

"Sure, hon."

We followed them into the office. Sally told Leanne and Carol about the flight. Leanne was grateful. She had stayed to catch any news. Icabod re-hung the first aid kit on the wall. Serge taxied in with a student in a Cherokee. Henry followed in the Super Cub. Sally plopped herself on the couch. Carol brought her a glass of water.

"If the twins had been born up there," Barry chuckled, "we could have named them 'Sky' and 'Hi'."

The joke caught Sally by surprise. She snorted water through her nose. Carol handed her a tissue.

"Are they boys or girls or both?" Leanne asked.

"We don't know," Barry answered.

"If they're one of each, you could call them 'Airy' and 'Merry'," Leanne said with a silly grin.

Sally snorted again. "Leanne, that's awful."

"I know. It's easy to name other people's kids. How about 'Up' and 'Down' or 'Hi' and 'Lo'?" our receptionist said with a laugh.

"Our poor children," Sally moaned.

"Or you could name them 'Sonny' and 'Moony'," I suggested.

"Oh, no," Sally exclaimed. She held her belly and tried not to laugh. Icabod joined the fun. "Maybe you could call them 'Air' and 'Mail'?"

"Or 'Will' and 'Fly'!" Leanne said.

"Call them 'Hi' and 'Jack'," I added.

We were all laughing by now, including Sally and Barry.

"Stop you guys!" Sally pleaded between giggles. She was holding her stomach as if it hurt to laugh but she couldn't stop. "Those names will stick," she groaned. "Ouch! Ooh! That smarts!"

"So, I guess 'Wing' and 'Nut' are out, too," I said.

"Ow! Barry! Ooh! This is more than giggle pain!" Sally exclaimed. She wasn't laughing anymore. "Ooh! There's another one! Barry, I'm not being funny! Ouch! They're not supposed to start this close together! Barry!"

"OK, let's go, hon!" Barry replied. "Hospital, here we come."

"I'll ride with you," Icabod said. He grabbed the first aid kit off the wall again.

"Here, take this," Carol said, shoving Sally's blanket under his arm."

Barry and I helped Sally off the couch and toward the door. Icabod ran ahead. Leanne held the door open. Sally couldn't stand up straight. She stiffened with pain about every third step.

"Ouch! Darnn, that hurt!"

"Hang on, dear, we're on our way!"

We half-helped and half lifted her to the station wagon. Icabod and I eased her into the back seat. Barry hopped into the driver's side and started the car. Icabod jumped in with Sally. I closed the door. They roared off to hearty cheers and cries of, "Good luck!" from a crowd of customers and staff standing behind me.

"It's a boy and a girl, both healthy," Barry reported by phone two hours later. "Sally is sore but fine. They are nine pounds each."

Carol had taken the call. "That's wonderful!" she declared. "Give her our best!"

She related the news to the rest of us in the office.

"Ouch! Better her than me!" I said.

"Maybe I can sell Barry an aerial banner announcement," Serge said with a grin.

"That's a great idea, Serge," Henry said. "Except make it a freebee."

"I can't earn commissions if you give the banner towing away," he said in mock complaint.

"Your contribution can be assembling the message," Henry replied.

"Speaking of making banners, where's Icky?" Serge asked.

"Barry said that he's walking back from the city," Carol replied.

Henry jumped up. "I'll see if I can catch him partway and give him a ride." On the way to the door, he looked at Carol. "Did Barry say what they're naming the babies?"

"Yes, he's calling the boy 'Abe' and Sally is naming the girl 'Bea'."

"Abe and Bea?" Serge repeated with a sour look on his face.

"I think we were doing better than that," I offered.

"The names are short for 'Above and Beyond'," Carol replied.

About the Author

Garth Wallace is from St. Catharines, Ontario, near Niagara Falls, where he learned to fly in a Fleet Canuck in 1966. From 1971 until 1990, Garth worked full time at various locations as a flying instructor, bush pilot and corporate pilot. It was during those flying years that he met the colourful characters and lived the humorous experiences that are the basis for his eight-book series of funny flying stories. Garth now lives near Ottawa, Ontario, Canada with his wife Liz. The author is available as an entertaining guest speaker.
Email: garth@happylandings.com
Web site: www.happylandings.com

About the Artist

Francois Bougie's interest in aviation was sparked at an early age by his father who restored several aircraft and constructed two homebuilts. Francois' passion led to a college education as an aircraft maintenance engineer and a career as an electro-mechanical designer in the aerospace industry in Montreal, Quebec. In the 1990s, Francois began applying an artistic talent to aviation art and industrial technical illustrations. His work has been published on several aviation book covers, posters and in aviation magazines. Francois is a licenced pilot. He has owned a Cessna 120 and a Pitts Special. He currently flies a classic 1946 Globe Swift that he restored.
Web site: www.bizzart.com

Other books by Garth Wallace

Wing Nuts is the eighth book in a series of hilarious flying stories written by Garth Wallace.
Below is more information on Wallace s other funny tales and additional aviation humour books published by Happy Landings.
Ordering information appears on page 208.

Fly Yellow Side Up

The hilarious story of a suburban pilot who moves north seeking the freedom and glory of flying floatplanes. Follow Wallace as he takes a bush pilot job with no floatplane experience and stumbles his way into the fascinating world of wilderness flying.

Soft cover

Pie In The Sky

*Laugh with Wallace as he learns that the riches to be found running a small-town flying school are not in the money but in the characters and the memories. In **Pie In The Sky** Wallace discovers cowboy agricultural pilots, Mennonite buggy buzzing and other off-the-wall adventures.*
Soft cover

Cockpit Follies

Student pilot Marathon Melville, aircraft salesman Skid Sicamore and a parking lot vigilante named "The Snitch" are some of the crazy characters in this hilarious book by Canada's leading aviation humorist, Garth Wallace.
Illustrated by Francois Bougie
Soft cover

The Flying Circus

Get ready to laugh again as Happy Landings presents more funny flying stories by Garth Wallace. **The Flying Circus** is a humourous tale of two instructors who start a flying school with loads of enthusiasm, little business sense and no money.
Illustrated by Francois Bougie
Soft cover

If Clouds Could Talk

The humour shifts to corporate aviation. Ride with Wallace as he flies eye-to-eye past the Statue of Liberty, radios a rhyming radar operator and learns aerobatic flying from a sadistic mortician.
Illustrated by Francois Bougie
Soft cover

You'd Fly Laughing Too

Fun tales of people up in the air in more ways than one. A Piper Super Cub joins Wallace s cast of crazy characters. The laughter builds as the author flies in and out of trouble around the industrialized Great Lakes, a region not ready for land-anywhere pilots. Soft cover
Illustrated by Francois Bougie

Also by Garth Wallace
Don't Call Me a Legend

The inspiring biography of Canadian aviation legend Charlie Vaughn who went from sky-gazing farm boy to world renowned ferry pilot. Fly with Charlie as he delivers a Cessna to Botswana, a Twin Otter across the Pacific and a Hawker Siddeley through Russia.
Hard cover

Also from Happy Landings
Papa X-Ray - Jim Lang

The true story of a trusty old airplane, a family adjusting to the far north and a greenhorn pilot flying in the ruggedness of Canada's Northwest Territories. Follow Jim Lang as he trades a trailer for an airplane and flies it as family transportation around the wilderness of Nahanni Butte. Soft cover

Magnetic North - *David Halsey*

Magnetic North chronicles a coast-to-coast trek across northern Canada by foot, dogsled and canoe. What started as the Trans-Canada Expedition became a gripping adventure for two young men who set out to rediscover the Canadian North the hard way.   Hard cover

---

Happy Landings books are available at pilot shops, aviation museums, book stores, gift shops or directly from the publisher.

Ordering information

Happy Landings accepts phone and fax orders with VISA or MasterCard, and mail orders with cheque, VISA or M/C

Telephone: 613-269-2552
Fax: 613-269-3962
Mail: Happy Landings
851 Heritage Dr. RR # 4
Merrickville, Ontario
Canada K0G 1N0
Internet: www.happylandings.com
E-mail: books@happylandings.com

Please mention if you would like your books by Garth Wallace autographed by the author